ALSO BY BRIAN DRAKE

BULLET ALLEY

SAM RAVEN
BOOK SEVEN

BRIAN DRAKE

ROUGH
EDGES
PRESS

*This one is for J-Rod, my technical advisor,
one heck of a fisherman,
and pal of many years.*

BULLET ALLEY

bullet alley

SHE WANTED TO DISTRACT HIM BUT SAM RAVEN SAW THROUGH her façade.

Jen Denosha faced him across the table in the quiet restaurant and talked and talked…about nothing. She talked about the uptick in sales at the defense company she and her husband David founded, her gardening; it was all a smoke-screen. Raven sat and listened, watching her animated expressions between sips of gin and tonic. He and David had once competed for Jen's affections; Raven lost.

She wasn't talking to catch up. She was filling space, her eyes distracted, and her movements in the chair—the subtle shifts, the adjustments to jewelry which needed none—were those of somebody trying to build up courage to get to the point. But Raven decided he was going to have to help her.

She was in the middle of blathering on about a new addition to their house. "…and then we had to deal with zoning issues, and the environmental people had to check the property to make sure there wasn't some endangered bug living on…"

"Jen."

She froze. She looked at Raven with a half-open mouth and startled eyes.

"Cut the shit."

And then Raven felt awful because her carefully made-up face broke into a grimace of pain and she started to cry.

Raven reached across the table. "Hey..."

"No, no, I'm sorry, Sammy." She waved him off and grabbed a tissue from her purse. She dabbed her eyes.

Raven and Jennifer Denosha were the same age, but she looked far better than his rough countenance displayed. If he had to put words to her description, she still had *it*, whatever *it* was, and considering she'd always had *it* Raven figured she worked extra hard to keep it now with age, nature, and gravity conspiring against her.

Her strapless dress fit tight around her body without looking like something she should have tossed after hitting 30; but the heavy make-up was odd to Raven. Piling on the crap wasn't her usual style. But who paid attention when she wore a diamond necklace and matching earrings which looked like they cost more than anybody in the restaurant made in a year?

They sat in a back corner booth with a light overhead, but the brightness was set low and created shadow companions in the confined space. Other patrons at the open tables on the main floor appeared cut off from them, albeit they shared the same general space; the privacy suited Raven. There wasn't anybody to stare at them as he and Jen shared their emotional moment.

She dried her eyes and didn't look at him.

"Jen—"

"I'm fine."

"Are you sure?"

She nodded.

"It's nice to see you," Raven said.

"Is it? Really?"

"Why would I lie, Jen?"

"Didn't I break your heart?"

"Twenty years ago. We were kids."

"You said some things."

"I said some awful things," Raven agreed. "I apologize."

She wiped her eyes with the back of her right hand and used her other to pick up the glass. Jen swallowed another mouthful of her drink.

"What's wrong, Jen?"

She let out a breath. "I left David. Took a pile of cash and got out. I'm heading to Barbados to figure things out."

"My goodness—"

"Don't, Sam." She bowed her head again. "I got tired of the act."

"And you wanted to meet me because—"

"I owe you an apology, too. I'm sorry I hurt you. Even if we were only *kids*. You know we weren't."

"Um…OK."

"Why do you say that?"

"It sounds like you've lived with guilt longer than I lived with hurt."

"You ass—"

"Hey. I appreciate your apology, it's nice to see you, I'm sorry you and Dave are kaput, and good luck in Barbados. But I don't think you asked me to meet you here only to apologize for being a young woman who wasn't in love with me."

More tears. Another tissue. *Dab dab.* She didn't want to ruin her make-up.

"I'm sorry I ever made your life as miserable as I've been most of mine, Sam."

"I still don't know why you're here."

"My husband."

"What about him?"

"I think he's selling secrets to foreign spies."

———————

RAVEN BLINKED. *Now* she had his attention.

And her visit made more sense.

"You've made a serious statement, Jen."

"I know."

Raven and Jen had known each other since the army, more years ago than Raven wanted to admit, but she'd worked in Army Intelligence while he handled duties in Special Forces. The third member of their club was David Denosha. When David and Jen left the army to get married, Raven continued to serve. Dave and Jen moved to California to establish a high-tech firm which eventually specialized in defense work and made them both rich.

But the idea of David selling secrets to foreign spies did not sit well with Raven. It wasn't the David Denosha he knew. The David he knew was a patriot through and through; he'd not even joke of selling information.

"I'm going to need to know more, Jen."

Her diamond earrings caught the overhead light and sparkled as she looked up. The tears were gone now. "We can't talk here."

"Where are you staying?"

She told him the name of her hotel.

"Let's go back to your room and talk," Raven said. "Did you drive here?"

"I took a cab."

"Finish your drink and I'll drive us to your hotel."

She swallowed what remained of her gin and tonic in one

gulp. The ice cubes clinked against her red lips; she dabbed her mouth after setting the glass down. Raven laughed as he finished his own. Some things never changed. Jennifer Denosha could still chug booze like a champ.

2

RAVEN SET THE LOCKS. WHEN HE TURNED, JEN THREW HER arms around his neck and kissed him hard.

He didn't stop her, but melted with her instead. Her mouth was warm, her breath scented with gin, and she hadn't been entirely wrong. He may have moved on with his life, but there were nights, lonely nights of quiet reflection, where she crossed his mind. He'd wonder what might have happened had she picked him instead of Dave, how *his* life might have been different considering the path he now traveled; he wondered what he might have done to keep her, or if it had been dumb bad luck.

But she was still officially married.

Raven pushed her away and held her at arms' length. They both needed a moment to catch their breath.

"Jen—"

"Please, Sam." Her eyes pleaded with him; a sheen of sweat covered her forehead. "David hasn't touched me in months. I need this."

She moved toward him. He held her back. "Jen—"

"Please! I'll tell you everything in the morning. Just give

me tonight." She kissed him again. Raven let twenty years of wonder and regret fall away as he scooped her off the floor and carried her to the bed.

RAVEN AWOKE to the sounds of Jen splashing in the shower. He glanced at the pile of clothes on the floor. His and hers. He'd have to put last night's clothes back on till he returned to his own hotel to change.

Cut the shit.

Yeah. Now *he* was trying to avoid the first obvious thought coming to mind. *You just slept with your old buddy's wife. Idiot.*

Worse, Raven didn't care. He hadn't said two words to David Denosha since he stormed out of their lives. But they *had* been close pals once, and excuses weren't Raven's style. He did it because Jen reminded him of what he might have been and wasn't. She was a fantasy of a totally different life path away from war without end. An attempt to recapture what he'd lost years ago. He reached for the locket he normally wore around his neck. The one he never opened, never talked about. It was gone. His neck was bare. He'd taken it off and put it on the nightstand beside the bed. He looked at the scuffed sterling silver and wondered. Had he ended up with Jen, he might not have the locket at all. Then again, it might be *her* picture inside instead of the other two currently residing within. His conscience. The ones he'd failed to protect.

Are you winning, son?

He listened more to the running water and wondered what was on her mind. She was leaving David. What had gone wrong? Funny. He didn't understand why he cared. But he did. For some reason. Raven scooted to the other side of the bed and grabbed the phone. She had promised to tell him everything over breakfast. He'd better get the food ordered so she wouldn't have long to wait once she finished.

Consulting the menu tucked into a small display near the phone, Raven ordered two Basic Breakfasts with extra sausage. There was a coffee maker with a tea option in the room, so Raven saw no need to ask for any—the tea bags provided came from a brand Raven liked. He hung up after the kitchen confirmed the order and gave him a delivery time.

"Good morning."

Startled, he looked over his left shoulder at Jen. She picked up last night's clothes and smiled at him. Without makeup, he finally saw her real face once again, the small birth mark on the side of her chin. She had nothing to hide using the face paint, except a few extra lines which had intruded without permission.

"Hi," he said.

"You okay?"

"Yeah."

"Shower's yours."

"Did you use all the hot water?"

"If it concerned you so much, you should have joined me." She laughed.

Raven raised an eyebrow. She'd tied a robe tightly around her with a towel wrapped around her head. She didn't say anything more as she finished collecting her dress, heels—the stuff from last night.

Last night.

Dammit.

"I ordered breakfast," he told her.

"Okay." Another smile. But she turned away as he climbed out of bed and, naked, stepped into the bathroom.

She had not used all the hot water, but midway, Raven switched to cold. *Snap out of it!*

Shivering, he turned off the spray, stepped out, dried off, glad for the steam covering the mirror. He had trouble deciding if he felt guilty or embarrassed or...what?

Enough!

He wasn't going to spend much time thinking about the past; there wasn't anything back there he wanted to deal with. Ever forward, don't look back. But now the past was getting dressed on the other side of the wall and he had nowhere to run this time.

Face it!

He wrapped a towel around his waist and exited. She had put his clothes on the bed and was packing her suitcase. She wore jeans and a tank top. And looked the same as Raven remembered twenty years ago, extra lines and all.

She stopped and looked at him. "Um—"

"What? I look better in the dark?"

Jen laughed. "I was thinking it's no fun to wear day olds."

"I'll live." He grabbed everything and dressed in the bathroom. By the time he finished, room service knocked on the door.

They sat on the room's small balcony overlooking the pool. The chilly morning kept other guests inside. The other balconies in view were empty.

The breakfast came in several Styrofoam containers. What they didn't balance on their laps they left on the deck or on the small table between the two chairs. Nobody had dining in mind when they built the balconies.

They ate without talking despite Raven's anxiousness to learn more about her accusations. He still didn't believe her. He needed evidence.

Finally, as they sat with Jen drinking coffee and Raven

tea, she said: "Well, I can't avoid it anymore. You want to know about David, don't you?"

"Yes."

"Denosha Defense has been working on next-generation missiles and bombs. Smaller, more efficient, you can pack more per plane than now. We call them *Venom Class*."

"Okay," Raven said.

"They're proprietary designs, and the plans for our air-to-air missiles are already on the black market."

"Uh-huh. Could the competition be trying to sabotage you? I'm sure a contract is a few billion dollars, right?"

"Try *ten billion*, Sam. They aren't plans *close* to what we're doing. They're the *exact* specifications."

"How did this happen?"

"I'm not sure. But I promise nobody's aware yet. The FBI hasn't shown up. I'd like you to sound the alarm. Maybe look into things yourself."

"How did you find out?" Raven said.

She sighed. "I saw an email to David, from a woman named Monique. She told him *the plans* were now in circulation. Then I queried some, uh, *friends* in low places, and they found them."

"And this Monique person—"

"She's French. David has taken up with a group of French people, he won't tell me who they are or what they have to do with the industry, and I think they're the ones behind all this. But I haven't been able to determine more. Monique comes to the house now and then. *Private* meetings."

"But you have no hard proof?"

She shook her head. "I'm not trying to jam him up. I'm not an angry wife trying to screw him over prior to a divorce. But the plans are out there and something isn't right with these French people."

"David and I didn't part on the best terms, Jen. We said things—"

She shut her eyes to fight back tears. "I know. I don't know who else to tell."

Raven tasted his tea. It was cold.

"What time do you leave?" he asked.

"Couple hours."

"You got a ride to the airport?"

"I was going to call a cab."

"I'll drive you," he said.

"Okay."

Raven let the conversation fade. He had no idea what to do. It might be better to pass the tip to the FBI and let them dig a little, but he doubted he'd convince them anymore than she had convinced *him*.

Because she hadn't.

3

THE ELEVATOR DESCENDED. IT WASN'T LONG BEFORE JEN BROKE the silence.

"If I wanted to hurt David, there are a ton of ways to do so without making up stores."

"I know," Raven said.

She took his right hand and gave it a squeeze. "Thanks for last night."

"Yeah."

"Maybe when I come back—"

"We'll see."

No roots. Nothing to tie him down.

Rule Number One. He only lived by two. He'd made the mistake of trying to break Rule One once. Never again.

"Sure." She let go of his hand.

The elevator slowed to a stop and the doors rumbled open.

RAVEN CARRIED her suitcases across the marble-tiled lobby to the front desk. They navigated an obstacle course of human bodies: incoming guests, other guests stepping out for sightseeing, and those patronizing the lobby sports bar. The buzz of conversation drowned out the music cranked over ceiling speakers.

She stopped to check out. He left the suitcase beside her and said he was going to bring the car around. She said okay. He kissed her cheek. She smiled. Raven started across the lobby for the exit.

Then a gun went off, crashing twice, the discharges echoing throughout the lobby. People screamed and began to run.

Raven spun around and registered two things:

Jen, bleeding, falling to the marble floor without a sound.

And a man in a leather jacket with dark hair, gun in hand, running for a side exit.

Raven bolted after the shooter. He stayed focused on the running man despite wanting to race to Jen. He knew she was gone.

Raven's shoes pounded on the tiled floor. He chased the killer into a hallway ending at a pair of double doors. They emptied into the plaza between the hotel and neighboring complex of shops, restaurants, and offices. *Too many people!* Rule Two: No gunfights in public. But now and then he had to break rule two despite the risk and this might be one of those times. But he had to catch the bastard first. He ran faster.

The killer, steps away from the doors, spun around. The flaps of his jacket flew open; he brought up the stainless revolver in his right hand. Raven dived, hitting the floor hard, sliding a little, then rolling behind a potted plant. The pot was half his height and almost as wide. The killer's shots whistled past. Raven peeked around the pot. The killer pushed open one of the doors and ran into the plaza.

Raven exited at speed and broke left, rolling onto the hot cement as the killer fired again. The slug whined off the pavement. Raven had anticipated the ambush, and now had more people screaming and running and blocking the killer from view. Raven put his feet under him and plowed through the crowd.

The plaza filled the wide space between buildings and branched off into a small park with more shops and restaurants before ending at a busy street. The killer ran for the park and the sloping steps leading to the road. Raven ran hard, legs and lungs straining, powered by rage. As the killer gained the steps, he tried taking two at a time. Raven reached him, grabbed for a leg, and the killer fell face first. He screamed as his face impacted with the edge of a concrete step. Raven grabbed a handful of the killer's black hair to smash his face a second time, but the killer kicked back. The blow landed in the center of Raven's gut and he doubled over, lunging again as the killer tried to get to his feet.

The killer breathed hard, dazed from the blow to his face; a cut across his nose leaked blood down to his mouth. Raven and the assassin swung at each other while trying to keep balance on the steps. Raven ducked a punch, slammed a fist into the killer's gut. The blow glanced off hard muscle. The killer swung again and scored. His fist connected with the side of Raven's head; he struck with a kick to Raven's knee next. Raven fell like a tree down the slope, his body bumping the corners of each step all the way to the smooth pavement at the base.

He gasped, his throat burning, pain filling his body. He struggled to rise, pressing his hands to the concrete and exerting force to raise his upper body from the ground. His muscles strained but failed to do the job. With a gasp he let his body go flat. He moved his legs a little, and reached for the steps. He crawled up the steps on his belly, dragging last night's clothes across the cement, stopping at the sidewalk prior to the street. The killer was gone but wouldn't be far if Raven hurried. He tried to push to his feet again but the gas ran out. He collapsed on the sidewalk.

Wailing sirens pierced his mental fog, but weren't loud enough to block out the thought which flashed to mind before he passed out.

Jen told me the truth.

RAVEN WOKE up on a hospital gurney in a noisy emergency room. A circular curtain kept him closed off from the other activity. A man sat in a chair beside the bed. He wore a gray suit and showed Raven a gold badge. The detective stood. He was tall, trim under his off-the-rack suit; bald; what little hair he had around his ears was gray. He had the wary eyes of a veteran cop, unasked questions brimming behind his eyes.

"I'm Detective Doyle, DC Metro." He spoke slowly. He wasn't in a hurry.

"Sam Raven."

"We know. We have questions, Mr. Raven."

"I do, too. You start."

Raven hurt all over, but his heart the most. Emotional pain overpowered physical every time.

"Witnesses say you engaged the shooter. Tell me what took place and why you chased him."

Raven told the detective about his reunion with Jen but none of what she had reported. He kept it general, two former lovers catching up when one happened to be passing through. Doyle asked why Jen had made a stop specifically in

Washington, DC prior to Barbados. Raven had no answer. Obviously, to see *him*, but Raven didn't live there. He had to fly in from Stockholm, where he lived on a houseboat, to meet her. Doyle didn't understand, and said so. Raven didn't understand, either, and fell back on the missed opportunity / broken heart routine. Doyle seemed satisfied, almost, with Raven's side. The person they really needed to talk about the stopover was in the morgue.

"Did she tell you somebody had threatened her, she was in danger, anything of the sort?" Doyle asked.

"No, Detective."

"Why did you chase the killer?"

"Look up my background and you'll know why."

"We did. What haven't you told me? Why was Mrs. Denosha traveling alone?"

"You'll have to ask her husband. He's in California."

"We will." Doyle put away his notebook. "Where are you staying?"

Raven told him.

"Don't go too far, Mr. Raven."

"The way I feel right now, I'm not going anywhere, Detective."

Doyle departed with a half-hearted good-bye and Raven stared at the encircling curtain. His jaw was tight; lips pressed together; fury in his eyes. War without end never allowed any peace. What moments he did have, he had to steal, and the ghosts of battles past always called him to duty before he was ready. Raven touched the locket around his neck; it was gone, but he found it on the table beside the bed next to his cell phone, wallet, rental car keys. He picked up the phone. Wiping his face, he sent a text message to his pal Clark Wilson at the Central Intelligence Agency. If he had to go back to war, he wanted all the information he could muster. The story about the Venom Class weapon system had to have made its way into CIA reports somehow.

Poor Jen. He'd lost her again, this time for reasons unknown. He had to honor her last request, and look into a story he hadn't believed at first, but certainly believed now. It took a murder to convince him. Of all life's possible ironies, this one stung the worst. He hadn't seen the killer coming, hadn't been able to protect her; the same fate as the pair whose pictures remained enclosed in his locket. Despite the rules he lived by, he'd fallen into a sense of normalcy, seduced by the idea he might be able to behave like a normal human being for a few minutes instead of a man on the edge of constant violence.

Now he'd learn the truth, and show somebody the meaning of *payback*. One way or another, some son of a bitch was going to pay, with his life, in return. He blinked when he realized it might not be a *man* he found; he had a woman named Monique to add to his suspect list. Who was she? Who were her friends? Why had Jen suspected them?

Answers would follow in time.

4

NURSES TENDED TO RAVEN'S CUTS AND SCRAPES, BUT HE HAD no broken bones or any other reason to remain at the hospital after sunset. He wanted to get back to his hotel and out of his day-old clothes. He wanted an ice-cold martini, maybe more than one, and time to himself in the peace and quiet of his room.

A cab brought him back to the hotel, and after a shower he dressed again and went out for a bottle of gin and other fixings. Back in his room, he mixed his drink and lay against the headboard staring at the wall. He was wrong about the peace and quiet. If he concentrated and sat still, the sounds of neighboring guests and activity in the hallway intruded on his solitude.

Such was life.

His cell rang. The ID said "Clark Wilson" and Raven answered with a groggy hello.

"You're on the police radar, old pal," Wilson said. "What's happening?"

Raven told him about the shooting.

"That was you?"

"Yeah, Clark."

"Where are you now?"

"My hotel." Raven gave him the name.

"Sit tight and don't drink all the gin. On my way."

Raven ended the call and dropped the phone beside him on the bed. He and Clark had a long history. They'd served in the CIA together for a few years after Raven left the army, but while Raven had gone his own way, Clark remained. He now served as a Senior Operations Officer for the Special Activities Center. He and Raven still helped each other from time to time, and Raven had done more than a few off-the-books favors for Clark in the years since he exited official government work.

Wilson knocked on the door twenty minutes later. Raven had a drink ready for him.

"Sorry it's in a paper cup," Raven said. The cups supplied in the room left *much* to be desired.

"It'll do." Wilson dropped into the chair beside the bed and angled himself so he and Raven could see each other. "Dare I ask?"

"Go ahead."

"How are feeling?"

"Awful, inside and out. I was going to call you anyway. This is a matter Uncle Sam might be concerned with."

"Tell me."

Raven related the story slowly, leaving nothing out but the intimate details between him and Jen. Wilson listened without comment and sipped his drink. He didn't reply until Raven finished speaking.

"We can try and get the hotel security footage, maybe get an ID on the shooter…"

"You'll raise a million red flags, Clark."

"What about a background check on Denosha? I can help there. Maybe we'll find something to connect with these French people she mentioned, though there will be a ton of women named Monique in Paris alone."

"There's never a Hortense when you need one." Raven surprised himself with the joke. He cracked a small smile.

"Jennifer had to have held back," Clark said. "For somebody to target her suggests she knew more than she let on. Hell, why'd she stop here anyway? Just to meet you?"

"Apparently."

"Did she suggest DC or were you already here?"

"I was at home," Raven said. "I flew in."

"She called and you flew across the ocean?"

"Yes."

"You have no idea how long she was here before you met up?"

"No. And if she had more to tell me, it died with her."

"What about her husband?"

"He's been informed by now. I thought I'd call him and see if we can talk."

"Good luck. I can dig a little into what Jen might have been doing here, but unless you find the connection in France, I'm not going to be much help."

"I get it," Raven said. "What do you know about this new missile system?"

"It's a big deal. Every major power wants more efficiency. More firepower for less or the same cost they're paying now. What we don't want is this stuff ending up in the hands of the wrong people. If the blueprints are in the wild, we can try and find them, or find who has them, and put a little pressure on to find out how *they* got them. Know what? I might be able to help more than I thought."

"It's the gin. Enhances thinking skills."

"Then refill my cup, old buddy."

Raven passed Clark the bottle.

———————

"DAVID, IT'S SAM. SAM RAVEN."

"My secretary told me—"

"I know what she said. You wouldn't have taken my call otherwise."

"Why *are* you calling, Sam?"

"I was with Jen the night before she died."

"You were *what*?"

"We had a drink. She told me you two were having trouble and she was on her way to Barbados."

"You spent the night with my wife."

"No, David." Raven shut his eyes. He hated lying. "We did *not* spend the night together. We had a drink and talked about the old days and a few other things. She was hoping you two might work things out after she had some time away."

"I don't believe you."

"David, I'm telling you the truth."

"And?"

"How about I meet you at the airport? I'll go with you to —" He had trouble forming the words.

"Get Jen's body?"

"Yes."

"How about you fuck off instead."

"Hey. Never mind how things turned out. You can't do this alone."

"I *will* do it alone, and I don't need *you*, Sam. Stay away. Jen never loved you anyway."

David Denosha hung up. The click sounded loud in Raven's ear. His hand shook as he set the cell phone down. He was numb inside despite the warm flush creeping through his body via his third paper cup martini. He hadn't said a word to David in twenty years and their first conversation was Raven calling to talk about David's dead wife.

Jen never loved you anyway.

No. Not true. David had been trying to hurt him. She had loved him once, even if only for a short time.

5

ON THE OTHER SIDE OF THE COUNTRY, DAVID DENOSHA SAT IN his office and tried not to turn over his desk in a fit of rage. He had to keep cool. His secretary was on the other side of the wall and she'd hear everything. What he wanted was to crawl into the back of a dark cave and vanish from the face of the earth.

He didn't want to be at work; his employees were talking about what happened behind his back. He had to tolerate their whispers and gossip, because they weren't the only ones watching. Monique and her crew were watching, too, and closely.

Denosha had made a deal with the devil.

He pushed back from his desk and turned to face the window behind him. The corporate office in San Francisco overlooked the Bay, with the massive Bay Bridge stretching across to the Oakland side with Treasure Island in between. The view usually calmed him during a stressful day, but nothing calmed the storm of emotions running through him after hearing Sam Raven's voice for the first time in twenty years.

The window glass partially reflected his face. It was a tired face, with green eyes, and he might have been handsome except for a crooked nose. He'd broken his nose twice while boxing in the army, and somehow had managed to make Jen his wife despite, in his mind, appearing more beast than beauty. Maybe it had worked out between them because of the dynamic; then again, in the end, it hadn't worked out at all. She'd left for good, and told him so. If she really said to Raven she only wanted time away to think, she'd lied to him.

Denosha tried to swallow but his throat was as dry as sand paper. He was upset about Jen's murder, yes, but he had also never expected her to leave Barbados alive.

And now with Raven involved, bringing back all the memories of the past, good and bad, he might have to prepare for Sam's murder, too.

They had to protect the *plan* at all costs. The fate of the world rested on the success of the plan. He knew it; his partners knew it. Jen had known the truth, too, but cold feet overcame good sense. She thought she might escape; dodge the target on her back; calling Raven was a last-ditch effort to throw everything back in their faces. *Well, check mate, hon.*

If Denosha hadn't agreed his wife was too dangerous to leave alive, he'd have been killed, too. By sacrificing Jen, he was really trying to save his own neck. As he avoided his reflection in the glass, his own accusing green eyes, he wondered if the choice had been the right one. He might not have saved himself at all. He may have only delayed the inevitable bullet in the head.

With a grunt he returned to his desk and pulled his cell from a drawer. The cell wasn't his personal phone. He used it only to contact Paris.

It was late in Paris, but the man on the other end of the line promptly answered.

"Yes?"

The voice was deep, and belonged to an older man. The voice carried weight. The man spoke with an undertone of authority Denosha had never challenged, nor had he seen anybody else stand up to his commands, demands, or instructions.

Well, except Monique.

"It's David."

"What is happening, David?"

Like the old bastard doesn't know. Denosha explained he'd be traveling to DC to get his wife's body. And he explained the call from Sam Raven, and how they might have a new problem.

"Mr. Raven is indeed a problem, David," the other man said. He spoke slowly, quietly, and his voice never lost its authoritative tone.

"You sound like you know more than me," Denosha said.

"According to the hotel security footage, Mr. Raven was in the lobby with your wife when our man pulled the trigger. Raven chased our man and wounded him, but he wasn't quite good enough. Our man escaped."

"Wait. Raven was at the hotel *with* her?"

"We do not know. All we know is he was present in the lobby. Perhaps he had offered to drive her to the airport. Such things happen, David. I understand the history between the three of you, but you have to give your friend *some* credit."

"Former friend."

"Not my concern, David. We have to go with the facts, and the *fact* is our man left a witness behind. We shall deal with him for failing to eliminate the witness. And, yes, we have to get rid of Mr. Raven, too."

Denosha let out a breath. "I'm leaving for DC on the first flight out tomorrow morning."

"I hope you have a pleasant flight."

Denosha blinked. *Old bastard sounds like he means it.*

The old man said good-bye and Denosha ended the call. He set down the phone and leaned against his desk. Finally, a choked sob surfaced. He shut his eyes tight, holding his breath, forcing the emotions back down to the depths.

If only Jen had been reasonable...

6

A KNOCK AT THE DOOR.

Raven wasn't expecting visitors. He turned off the television and left the big chair by the bed to answer the door.

Detective Doyle. Blue suit this time; same wary eyes and weathered face.

"Hello, Detective."

"We need to talk."

Raven stepped back and the detective entered, scanning the room, facing Raven when he found nobody else within. His glance barely lingered on the television; Raven had been mindlessly flipping channels, and settled on a cooking show. He was thinking about how he hadn't been doing much of his own cooking lately when the detective knocked.

Doyle removed his pocket notebook and consulted a page.

"Where were you today?"

"What do you mean?"

"I mean where were you today? What did you do after you got out of bed this morning?"

"Do I need a lawyer?"

"Do you?"

"Tell me what this is about or arrest me, Detective," Raven said. "I was here in the room all day resting. Hotel security cameras will confirm I never left via any of the four or five exits from the lobby."

Doyle flipped back two pages in his notebook. "We found a body this morning, Mr. Raven. A man with a gash across his nose, black hair, wearing a leather jacket with a .357 Magnum in one of the pockets. He fits the description of the man who shot Jennifer Denosha."

"Oh," Raven said.

"And you haven't left the hotel all day?"

"Check the cameras. I didn't even go downstairs for breakfast; ordered room service."

"I'll check." Doyle closed his notebook. "Thank you." He turned for the door. "You make sure you stay put, Mr. Raven." Doyle opened the door and let it swing closed behind him. Raven set the locks and returned to his cooking show, but found he was no longer interested. He turned off the television and called Clark Wilson to give him the update.

"Wow," Wilson said. "Hang on, let me log in and see if I can access the police report."

Raven listened while Clark tapped the keyboard of his computer. After a few minutes, the CIA man said, "They found the body in an alley. The alley wasn't where he was killed. He was only dropped there. Somebody shot him twice in the chest. Nine-millimeter. You haven't changed guns, have you?"

Raven still packed his .45 pistol and said so.

"No sign of torture so it's safe to say nobody worked him over before whacking him," Clark said. "Works in your favor."

"Gee. Thanks." *Though he isn't wrong...*

"Nobody pops an assassin for no reason, Sam."

"Whatever is happening is big, I agree."

"And if they tagged the killer—"

"They'll be looking for me."

"Did you talk to Denosha?"

"He doesn't want me around," Raven reported. "Once I see him in person, I think he'll cool off. He's in shock."

"So are you."

"Yeah."

"Get some rest. You looked like hell yesterday and probably still do."

"Haven't bothered with a mirror today so I couldn't tell you."

They said good-bye and Raven sat on the edge of the bed. Jen's story was proving true, more and more, with each passing event. What did David know, when had he known it, and what was his overall responsibility in the matter? Was he the mastermind, or marching to somebody else's drum beat? Was he manipulated via blackmail or other means? If David was as much a victim as Jen, maybe Raven could convince him to visit the FBI and go on record. And if he *was* the mastermind, Raven would take care of the problem himself. But unlike whoever murdered Jen's killer, there'd be no body left behind for cops to find.

DAVID DENOSHA DIDN'T REGISTER the length of his cross-country flight. He sat in his first-class seat in a daze. The last 24 hours had drained him, but he fought off sleep. He didn't want to see Jen in his dreams. Only the flight attendant assigned to his section yanked him from the trance, and only then to offer him a drink or collect his empty cup. If she recognized a businessman with a lot on his mind, she gave no evidence.

Denosha looked out the window and thought about better times. About Jen when they were younger. How they'd parlayed their military careers into building one of the largest defense manufacturing firms in the United States. It had been her company as much as his. They'd worked together, struggled together, conquered together. They'd made a good team until the problems and arguments began; before disgust at each other's presence took over.

And then Denosha developed ideas about who should have advanced weapons and who should not. He found simpatico thinking when he met Monique, and the old Frenchman in Paris. Jen agreed—at first.

Denosha examined the countryside far below. It rolled like a canvas from a scroll and didn't seem real at altitude. But it was very real indeed. There were people down there whom Denosha had pledged his life to protect; the deal with the Frenchman was an extension of his youthful oath of service. But it took a special mindset to understand.

He shifted his thoughts to Sam Raven.

He'd hurt Raven almost as much as Jen after they tied the knot. He hoped Raven might get over it. David and Jen didn't cut off contact after sharing angry words over the phone; Raven did. Why had Jen gone to him after so much water under the bridge? How had she even known how to find him? The only way was through one of the intelligence databases they accessed for work. She had specifically *sought him out*.

She knew *everything*. How much did she tell him? Had Raven believed her? If not, he surely did now. After talking to the Frenchman, Denosha checked Raven's recent history on his own, and learned enough to make him nervous. Raven was still a shooter, albeit freelance, and it meant he still knew how to handle himself. If Raven believed Denosha had anything to do with Jen's death, now *David* had a target on his back and his old buddy held the gun.

David Denosha suddenly felt very tired inside and out, more so than earlier; a sense of dread settled over him. No way to shake it off. He had a mission. Pick up Jen's body, get her home for burial. Play the role of grieving widow. He was. To a point.

When the flight attendant announced their final descent into Dulles, he brightened a little. All he had to do was stick to the plan. The Frenchman knew how to handle problems like Sam Raven.

7

RAVEN WASN'T SURE WHAT HE'D SAY TO DAVID. BUT HE STILL had time to figure out at least the first few words. He waited near the baggage carousels at Dulles, watching the digital readouts displaying airline and flight numbers. He stood at the second of three rotating carousels with American 305 displayed. The first flight from SFO in California. Raven had no idea if David was aboard or not; he likely was. If not, he planned to wait until David eventually showed up. When he saw David cut through the crowd and approach the carousel, he grinned. Despite the years gone by, David, like his late wife, hadn't changed much.

Raven worked around the gathered crowd and stopped a few feet from David.

"Dave."

Denosha snapped his eyes to Raven in surprise. His frown turned into a smile. For Raven, the years of animosity and anger faded. His friend had lost his wife, and Raven wanted to help him through the grieving process. Then he checked himself. Helping his pal as all well and good, but he had

another agenda, too. Getting to the truth of what Jen had
told him.

"Sam."

A warm handshake turned into a hug. They weren't
divided by a woman any longer. They were two army vets
who'd met the first day of basic training and found a variety
of ways to get drunk, raise hell, and serve their country.

They looked at each other, both nervous, uncertain, and
Raven tried to talk but had trouble finding the right words.
Start with the basics.

"I'm sorry, David. Really."

"Thanks. I missed you, bud."

"It's been too long."

There was more to say, but not within hearing range of
others. Denosha collected his single suitcase and followed
Raven out to a rental car. Raven paid the parking fee and
drove through the exit gate. On the road, Denosha further
broke the ice.

"This isn't supposed to be happening."

"No." Raven cleared his throat. He knew what his friend
was going through. He'd been through the same thing once.

A long time ago.

"Look, Dave, a long time ago I said some things…"

"All's forgiven. We both said things. We're both going
through hell right now." Denosha paused a moment. "What
makes it worse is the goddamn funeral home—"

"What about it?"

"They gouge you when dealing with a surprise death. Talk
about charlatans who should be prosecuted."

"I hear you."

"But I have a nice spot picked out for her. She'll be overlooking the ocean."

"You're going to cremate her?"

"Yes." Denosha choked out the word and went silent.

Raven drove and didn't talk, either. Going through hell, indeed. He was running an op on his old friend; as he sat behind the wheel, he wondered again if Jen had told the truth. Or maybe she had, but misrepresented Dave's role. Maybe he was a pawn in somebody else's scheme.

And Raven wondered if he was fooling himself.

Denosha wiped his eyes with a handkerchief and cleared his throat.

"Where are we going?"

"Away from the airport. What hotel are you staying at?"

Denosha told him. Raven made a course correction at the next freeway exit.

"So," Denosha said, "you married?"

"Not anymore."

"Oh, no, I'm sorry."

"Don't worry about it. Jen said your company is doing well. Designing some new missiles or something? She was vague."

"It will be a big deal if we get the contract. Lockheed and Grumman are also bidding; they're the big shots."

"You'll be fine."

"It's not as fun as it used to be," Denosha said. "I manage and I schmooze clients. I don't build and design anymore. I didn't get into business to manage and schmooze. I wanted to build stuff."

"Life does that to us. Does we get what we want, or do we only go with the flow?"

Raven slowed to pull up at Denosha's hotel. David insisted Raven join him for a drink. Raven waited in the bar while Denosha dropped his luggage in his room, and ordered for them both.

When Denosha joined him, they sat in a corner booth. One drink followed another as they reminisced about the old days and forgot about the circumstances which tore their friendship apart and brought them together again. Eventually, Denosha called it a night; Raven, too sloshed to drive, booked a room for the night, too.

"We gotta get my wife tomorrow," Denosha said in the elevator. Sadness crossed his face. "It's funny..."

"What?" Raven asked.

"For once she has to be somewhere and she won't be late."

Denosha laughed through a sudden burst of tears. Raven felt it, too.

THEY DIDN'T TALK on the plane.

Both were heavy with the knowledge of Jen's coffin riding in the cargo hold. Raven sat in the middle seat and let David stare out the window. Raven pretended to read a paperback western. He couldn't focus on the words. His thoughts were instead centered on what he and David had said last night; more important, what they hadn't.

Neither had talked about Jen or her murder. Raven hadn't mentioned the dead killer or Detective Doyle, who would *not* be happy Raven took off, but he'd deal with the cop later if need be. He didn't want David to know he knew more than he did. But he wondered if David already knew what he knew. There had been moments, while they'd been drinking, Raven had caught a suspicious glance on Denosha's face.

The good feelings regarding David weren't fake, but he had to compartmentalize his competing thoughts, those of the *mission*.

He'd packed his war tools for the California trip. One of his suitcases contained an X-ray proof compartment; nestled inside was Raven's Nighthawk Custom Talon .45 autoloader, a set of spare magazines and ammunition, and a speed rig shoulder harness. He hoped he didn't have to use the weapon. But he knew he'd have to. Maybe even on David.

DENOSHA STARED out the window because it kept him from looking at Raven.

He had to be careful. He had to not lose sight of the goal.

The plan. It was all about the *plan*.

The countryside hadn't changed since his last pass. Or perhaps it had—a different perspective going the other way. All he knew for sure was he couldn't bring himself to ask Raven what Jen told him. Raven hadn't disclosed anything, either. He, in fact, didn't seem to have any idea. Why the old buddy act if he knew the truth? If he didn't know anything, maybe Denosha had a way to convince the Frenchman to lay off. Too many dead bodies connected to one another wasn't a good idea—eventually, the Feds would start asking questions. And snooping Feds might derail the plan as fast as Raven in full assault mode.

There was only one way to find out, if he was willing to ask. The Frenchman's killer had been watching Jen. Denosha and Raven might have been under surveillance in DC, too. A chill crawled up Denosha's neck. If the Frenchman decided *he* was a threat, too...

He looked at Raven reading his book. If he came clean, maybe Raven could help? Wait, help with what? No, he could only stick to the plan. The Frenchman had too many connections all over the world. If Denosha went rogue, there'd be nowhere for him to hide.

Back to the window. *Watch the scenery*. He'd have to wait and see. Give it a little more time.

8

A HEARSE ON STAND-BY COLLECTED JEN'S COFFIN WHEN THE plane landed. Raven and Denosha watched as attendants from the funeral home loaded the coffin into the back, and joined the driver up front.

Raven and Denosha loaded their suitcases into a company car and climbed inside. The hearse drove away to the funeral home; Denosha's car went the opposite way. When they reached Highway 101, Denosha let out a sigh.

"Funeral tomorrow," he said.

"Yeah," Raven said. The rear seat of the Lincoln Town Car was covered in soft leather. It should have been a comfortable ride, but Raven felt anything but. He was following his old friend into a lion's den, and only Denosha knew all the exits.

"You're invited to stay with me, Sam. Don't bother with a hotel. I could use the company."

Raven decided he didn't want to be alone, either. And if he was inside Denosha's place, lion's den or not, he could poke around. He waited a moment before answering, then said: "Sounds fine."

"We're going to my place in South San Jose. Got a big spread. You'll have a guest cottage to yourself."

"Wow."

"Seems a bit worthless now with Jen gone, but it was our sanctuary."

An hour into the drive, Raven remarked the "sanctuary" was also very far away.

"The whole point," Denosha said, "was to get away from all this crap."

He gestured out the tinted windows at the passing urban spread. Apartment buildings and condo complexes dominated one side of the freeway; large shopping areas and restaurants covered the other side, with plenty of bright signs announcing who was who.

"Where we're at," Denosha continued, "we're surrounded by farms. Peace and quiet. You'll love it."

Raven nodded and let his mind wander over the same thoughts he'd been cycling since Jen died. He tried to find solace in their last moments together, but there hadn't been any real intimacy there. They were a pair of broken wings grabbing for comfort.

All he felt when thinking about Jen was guilt.

All he wanted when thinking about Jen was revenge.

_____

"HOW OFTEN DO you make this drive, Dave?"

"Getting bored?"

The view out the windows went from urban sprawl to fields and grassy hillsides.

Raven laughed. "A little."

"I don't notice it anymore. Long distances between two points in the Bay Area, home, office, all that, is normal."

"This is longer than Richmond to DC."

"Sure."

"You're crazy, but whatever makes you happy."

"The house is worth the wait. Trust me. I'll get dinner going for us, okay? Few beers, too."

"We both need a few beers, yeah."

TWENTY MINUTES later the Town Car drove through the gate of the Denosha "sanctuary". Raven whistled. The two-story house occupied major space in the center, with two smaller cottages off to the left. The rest of the property contained a variety of plants, flowers, immaculate patches of grass. Small security lights lit the grounds.

"It looks better when the sun is up," Denosha said.

"I bet."

Denosha unlocked one of the guest cottages and told Raven to make himself comfortable while he put steaks on the grill. Raven shut the door after Denosha exited. The cottage wasn't huge, but might as well have been a studio apartment. Bed, sitting area, television on the wall, small patio shared with the second cottage overlooking a portion of the garden. Raven went to work unpacking. He needed clothes for the funeral, and while he had a decent outfit among the packed collection, none were in basic black. Raven left his gun in the bottom of the suitcase. He didn't want to think about needing the hardware for a while.

RAVEN EXAMINED HIS PHONE. He looked at the screen as if he expected the device to talk to him, to suggest he get on with disagreeable work. He wasn't somebody who liked to live in the past. His past held too many personal demons—mental, of his own imagination; and real, people who had come and gone from his life, sometimes violently, sometimes not. He'd already faced one in the form of Jen; now, he was going to bring another back into his life, somebody he had thought had passed into the ether, never to be seen again, fit only for a man's reflections.

Raven selected a name from his contact list and dialed. He listened to the other line ring and waited for a woman named Kayla Blaine to answer.

The last time he visited San Francisco, he'd done so to bust a US-French drug connection involving local mafiosi— who no longer breathed good air. They were worm food and the world was better off with their absence. At the time, Kayla Blaine had been a San Francisco cop caught in the middle and on the run. Thanks to Raven, she survived, and now worked for the Federal Bureau of Investigation.

She answered curtly.

"This is Kayla."

Raven paused. If he was going to pull her into the case, he had better be ready for potential consequences.

What if he failed to save her, too?

"Hello?" she prompted.

"It's…" He cleared his throat. "Kayla, it's Sam Raven."

"Um…what?"

The fight against the drug alliance pushed the two of them together in unexpected ways; they'd been lovers for a short time, and she'd wanted him to stay. He couldn't. *No roots.* She hadn't understood then; maybe she did now.

"Sam Raven," he repeated. "I'm in South San Jose. I need your help on something. Can I see you?"

"You're here on a job?"

"Yes."

"Like last time?"

"I hope not," he said. "But it will involve the FBI if it goes bad, so I thought I'd call you."

"How did you know I was FBI now, Raven?"

"I keep an eye out."

"When do you need to see me?"

"Tomorrow sometime. I'll let you know. I have a funeral in the morning."

"Related to—"

"Yes," he said.

"All right. Call me when you can and we'll talk about it."

"Okay."

"It's good to hear your voice again," she said. "Been quiet without you around."

Raven laughed a little. "You're better off, Kayla. See you tomorrow."

"Hey," she said. "Don't go charging around like a bull. Not without me, anyway."

"See you tomorrow," he said again.

"For sure."

She hung up and Raven put the phone on the nightstand. He was smiling a little.

The rumble of a car engine intruded on his thoughts. He went to the patio doors. The car drove through the main gate and up to the front of the house. Black Mercedes, tinted windows—he had no way to see inside. Then it didn't matter because a woman climbed out of the back and shut the door. The driver did not leave the car. The woman was dressed smartly in a long skirt and blouse combo, dark colors, requisite heels and leather purse. Tall, narrow hips, long black hair, and a stern expression. She might have been the mysterious Monique referred to by Jen as a regular visitor to the house. Raven regretted not asking for a description when he had the chance. But his gut told him it was her.

The woman went up the steps to the front door and out of Raven's sight.

9

Denosha stood in his private office with a bottle of whiskey in one hand and a glass in the other. The front door opened and closed and he frowned. He didn't think Raven would have unpacked so quickly. He poured into the glass while yelling, "I'm upstairs!"

But Raven didn't enter the room. Monique Choffron stepped through the doorway. She did not look happy, but Resting Bitch Face was a normal thing for her. She fixed her dark eyes on Denosha and said, "Pour a lady a drink?"

"Show me a lady." Denosha set the glass on the bar and retrieved another from the shelf in front of him. She collected the first glass while he poured the other. On the couch, Monique crossed her legs and gave him a smile as warm as a crocodile's snort. Denosha's pulse quickened, but not in a good way. He remained standing by the bar.

"We have a few things to talk about, David."

"Like what?" He sipped his drink. Her face appeared distorted through the glass as he lifted it to his lips.

"Why bring your friend here?"

"Are you watching the place?"

"How can we deal with him if he's so close? What might he discover while he is here? Have you thought about any of this, David?"

"The best way to deal with Sam Raven is to leave him alone. We start leaving dead bodies all over the place, and somebody is going to notice."

Monique laughed and finally swallowed some of her drink. "We can't leave him alive."

"All this will go away after tomorrow, when he leaves. He doesn't know anything."

"She spent time with him. She told him. There is no other reason to get Raven involved. He's not going anywhere until he has answers."

"No, Monique. Leave him to me."

"What did Raven tell you they talked about?"

Denosha gave her a rundown of his catch up with Raven, and she shook her head when he finished.

"No," she said. "I don't believe him."

"Suit yourself." Denosha swallowed the contents of his glass in one throw. He turned to set the glass on the bar; when he turned back, Monique stood in front of him. She put a hand on his chest. He froze. She turned him around to face the bar, setting her half-empty glass down, and began to massage his shoulders.

"Oh, you poor thing. You're in bad shape. Very tense and angry."

The left corner of Denosha's upper lip twitched; his eyes landed on her glass. He grabbed it, twisting around, and tossed the remains in her face. She recoiled at the impact; some droplets struck him, too.

"Bitch! Fucking *whore*! You murdered my wife!"

Fury covered Monique's face. At the couch, she found her purse, and took out a handkerchief with which to pat her face dry.

"You'll pay for this, David.'

"Get out."

One last wipe over her eyes and nose and she returned the handkerchief to the purse. "We'll see what the partners have to say about this."

She pivoted and marched out of the room. Denosha stared at the doorway long after she'd gone.

IN THE GUEST COTTAGE, resting on the bed, Raven heard the car start. He stood up and watched from the patio door again as the car made a U-turn and departed the way it arrived.

He was sure it was Monique. Another testimony to Jen's truthfulness.

Hello, Monique. Nice to meet you.

I'm going to kill you later.

MONIQUE FUMED in the back seat of the Mercedes. She'd never seen Denosha fly into a rage before, and for him to attack her...well, it was obvious the murder of his wife had taken a toll, one of those matters one might understand theoretically but object to in real life. And reality had hit Denosha square in the solar plexus.

They should have taken out *both* of them and started fresh with another defense company. There were plenty available; the world did not rotate around the sun simply because David Denosha existed.

She used her cell phone to dial Paris. The old man answered right away.

"What is it?" the Frenchman said.

"David is departing the reservation. The stress has broken him. He's upset and unstable."

The Frenchman said nothing. Usually his silence meant disagreement, but Monique wasn't going to let him influence her.

"He is no longer of use to us," she said. "He must be eliminated. We never should have left him alive to begin with."

"Why the sudden change?"

"Really? You have a lot to learn about human nature. It doesn't matter if he and his wife weren't getting along. She was still his wife."

The Frenchman ignored her. "Does Mr. Raven have something to do with the change?" the Frenchman asked.

"Denosha might be thinking of a confession, if so," Monique said.

"Perhaps you're right. It's time to cut our losses. The mater will be settled shortly. Thank you, Monique." The Frenchman hung up.

Monique cracked a smile. Yeah, David was going to pay dearly. And with his life.

10

SMOKE FLOWED FROM THE SIDE STACK ON THE OUTDOOR GRILL, filling the air with the aroma of sizzling beef. Raven held a bottle of beer and watched Denosha turn the steaks. He noted David's look of...what? Exhaustion. If Raven hadn't known better, he'd have called it a combat stare, the dull expression, the unblinking eyes. Denosha was barely holding on and Raven didn't blame him, but was it because he knew the truth, or because he didn't? If he didn't, Raven wondered how to approach the question of soliciting David's help. Because *somebody* was behind the killing.

"Want me to take over, Dave?"

"Huh?"

"Let me take over. You look like hell"

"I feel like hell."

"Come on, sit at the table, let me finish, and we can try to enjoy the night."

"Fat chance."

"I know. Humor me."

Denosha grabbed his beer and plopped onto a chair. The small patio table wobbled a little as Denosha set his bottle down. The night air was cool and the patio space behind the house wasn't cluttered. To Raven, it felt lifeless. Generic furniture rested on a slab of concrete. The grill, coated with dust on the outer shell—barely used, never cleaned. The wobbly table. Raven would have figured Denosha and Jen to splurge on a nice set up. But he wasn't going to ask. They either hadn't used it much, so why bother, or cooked outside to bring food inside, or it was a project David never scratched off the to-do list and now probably had no intention to finish because why bother?

Raven shut the grill lid, drank more beer, and joined Denosha at the table.

"You gonna say it?" Denosha asked.

"Say what?"

"This patio looks like crap."

"I wasn't going to say anything at all," Raven said.

"Well, it sure does, doesn't it? It was on my list of things to fix up, but you know. Business and all that."

"Sure." Raven swallowed what was left in his bottle. Denosha jumped up to grab two fresh bottles. He sat again and placed the full one in front of Raven. Raven snapped off the top. Denosha let his sit.

"There were a lot of things we were going to do," Denosha said. "Then the arguments began, we stopping getting along, drifted apart. I'm sure she filled you in."

"I told you, Dave. She only said she was going—"

"Yeah, yeah, Barbados." Denosha dismissed the remark with a wave. He looked pained. He displayed a grimace, as if he'd swatted at a fly and missed and now it was buzzing over his head. He drank down his beer and opened the second bottle.

"I tell you what I got here," Denosha said, "is one heck of a security system."

"Do tell." Finally, a change of subject. The more Raven

had to deny anything happened between him and Jen, the more he was afraid he'd slip.

"We went all fancy. Little cameras all over. Every corner of the roof, a couple on the wall, they're small, hard to see unless you're up close. The alarm system puts an electronic screen around the place, crisscrossing invisible lines; if one is interrupted, the alarm goes off."

"And if a bird lands or a cat comes onto the property?"

"Built into the system. Multiple lines have to be tripped."

"Got a server in the house to store what the cameras record?" Raven asked.

"It all goes to the cloud. I can view footage from here, my office, my *other* office"—he laughed—"anywhere. I don't need to have a server room."

Raven left his chair and lifted the grill lid. "These are done, Dave."

"Then let's eat. I'm tired of talking."

Raven agreed.

THEY ATE QUIETLY, each cutting his steak with efficiency, washing down the meat with mouthfuls of beer.

Raven knew there were questions he shouldn't ask, at least at the moment, but he did want the answer to one question in particular.

"Who was the woman who showed up?"

"You saw her?" Denosha's eyes widened a little.

"I saw her from the patio window, yeah."

Denosha sliced another piece of steak, taking his eyes off Raven as he did so. "Somebody from work. Wanted to see how I was doing."

Raven didn't believe him, but there was no sense in

arguing until he had more information. But he wondered, still, what the woman's business had *really* been.

After dinner they carried the dishes inside and piled everything in the kitchen sink. Denosha didn't feel like cleaning up, and told Raven to leave everything till after the funeral. His voice caught when he said the word. Raven didn't stop him from going up to his room. He returned to his cottage for his own solitude.

DENOSHA SLEEP-WALKED through the funeral with dark glasses concealing his eyes. He made the necessary remarks to attendees but left most of the eulogy presentation to the minister, and friends of Jen who wanted to remember her with stories and anecdotes.

Like any funeral, it was a depressing affair, this one especially so considering the circumstances, and Raven stuck close to Denosha for support but didn't engage with any guests. The wake at a restaurant in San Carlos remained muted, but stories of Jen continued, and Raven had a sense of catching up on the parts of her life he'd missed. The knowledge only deepened his sense of loss.

The wake over, Raven and Denosha returned to the house where Denosha traded funeral clothes for jeans and a T-shirt and cleaned the dishes from the night before. He told Raven he didn't want help, and Raven remained in his cottage watching television to pass the time. And think.

He wasn't learning anything through observation. Despite their problems, Denosha behaved like a man genuinely grieving. It wasn't an act. He didn't doubt Jen's story but once again questioned David's actual role. He'd try another tactic. Tell David the truth. Not about his night with Jen, Raven would take those moments to his grave, but about what Jen told him regarding the Venom missile system and the plans leaking to the black market. If David wasn't involved, he'd want to help when he learned the truth. Raven would feel better with backup. *Motivated* backup.

After a night's rest, Raven decided to see how David would react to the story.

He forgot to call Kayla.

11

DAVID DENOSHA HAD NO INTENTION OF SETTLING DOWN FOR the evening until he knew if Raven had talked to anybody since his arrival.

What he'd neglected to tell Raven regarding his fancy security system was that it extended to the cottages. Each of the guest houses were wired for sound. Bugged. Sitting on his bed with a laptop, Denosha clicked on the sound file associated with Raven's room. Unless Raven made a habit of talking out loud to himself, Denosha didn't think there'd be much. But if Raven made any phone calls, he'd at least have a one-sided conversation on which to base his next move.

He found a file. Raven *had* made a call. Denosha listened.

"Kayla...it's Sam Raven...yes, I hope not. But it will involve the FBI if it goes bad...I keep an eye out...Tomorrow sometime. I'll let you know. I have a funeral in the morning... Yes...Okay...You're better off, Kayla. See you tomorrow..."

Denosha closed the file. Raven hadn't gone anywhere yet, or made another call. Maybe he was putting it off a while. He frowned.

FBI.

Why was Raven talking to an FBI agent?

Raven wasn't leaving, despite what Denosha told Monique about his visit being temporary. He knew *something*. Jen had told him about the plan, the French syndicate, *something*. The *old buddy* act was exactly an act, put on by a master showman.

Denosha frowned. Was he any different? He was putting on a show, too, for his own ends. There was no sense in being a hypocrite about it. They were both trying to fake each other out. But there also had to be *some* genuine good will on the surface, if only on the *surface.*

Denosha placed the laptop on the nightstand and stood to pace around the room. Was there a way to lead Raven to a conclusion different from what Jen described—assuming she told him everything about the plan. *Assume he knows it all.* How might he steer Raven to the three people at the company associated with the plan, while at the same time keeping himself clear of any of his old pal's suspicions?

There were flaws in the thinking. Denosha recognized the problems right away. Anybody caught by Raven and his FBI friend would in turn testify against Denosha.

Trying to shift the blame wasn't going to work.

Unless...

Unless he showed the syndicate the value in such a distraction, solicited their help, and let the other three take the fall. If they blamed him, he could claim they were trying to frame him. There was no paper trail linking Denosha to the other three involved; their word against his, with evidence to prove they were acting alone...

Anything to save your own skin, right, Dave-O?

In the fallout, Denosha might find a way to get out entirely, with the money he'd socked away, and hide somewhere to live out the rest of his days in quiet exile.

But Raven isn't stupid. He'll figure it out!

54 | BRIAN DRAKE

Another potential problem. But avoidable if the syndicate agreed; *if* the Frenchman hadn't been convinced by Monique, after his outburst, that he was no longer a *team player*. Offering a scheme to not only protect *him* but the rest of the group, and the *plan*, might work in his favor. They had to understand whacking a bunch of people wasn't going to keep the plan a secret.

He had to try. Worst case, he fell on Raven's mercy. Find a reason to show he'd been blackmailed, duped, threatened, etcetera. There were ways. *Use the old buddy act.* Raven wasn't stupid, but he had emotional blind spots like anybody else. If he was so fixated on renewing formerly dead friendships, he might go for the act.

Denosha took a deep breath and stopped pacing. The mental exercise had drained him, and after a shower he gratefully climbed into bed for the remainder of the afternoon. But sleep eluded him. There had once been somebody lying beside him, and she wasn't there any longer.

RAVEN ANSWERED his cell with a groan, which turned into a yawn and a mumbled hello.

"You okay?" Clark Wilson said.

"Dozed off." He sat up against the headboard.

"Want me to call back?"

"No. We can talk." Raven swung his legs over the side of the bed and stood. The closed drapes let in slivers of afternoon light. "What's going on?" He started moving to get the gears turning. The fog of sleep started to clear.

"I have a few updates from our last conversation. Jen Denosha and her movements prior to seeing you, as well as—"

"Start there."

"I checked on her arrival in DC to the time you met her at the restaurant," Clark said. "Our question was whether she saw anybody else, or did anything else, prior to seeing you. The answer is no. She did not."

"How do you know?"

"She checked into the hotel ninety minutes after landing at Dulles, which accounts for collecting luggage and her cab ride in traffic. It puts her at the hotel at a quarter after five in the evening. You two met at—"

"Six-thirty."

"I think she had just enough time to get ready to meet you. She didn't fly with her little black dress and make-up on."

"I'm inclined to agree, pending any new information."

"She had a plan only to see you, Sam. I'd bet on it."

"Okay." Raven wasn't sure what he thought about the information. He'd hoped she *had* left something behind; or had another contact who might fill in the gaps. But the window of time available didn't suggest she'd had the chance.

Raven couldn't make sense of *why*. Why him? What was so special about *him* to make her take a detour on her way to Barbados?

Raven shook his head. He was running in circles, dulled with heartache, and not helping himself by chasing rabbit trails.

"Are you there, Sam?"

"I'm listening."

"Cops are wondering where you're at. Somebody named Doyle, specifically."

"He can find me later."

"Local FBI made the connection between Jen and her husband, and I understand they've already been in touch with the local Feds in your area. You may see one or two snooping around."

"I have an FBI contact here. She might have been assigned."

"She?"

"Long story," Raven said.

"Watch your ass. They've been told you left in the middle of the investigation and may be a person of interest, though Doyle admits he has no reason to hold you for anything."

"I'll be careful."

"The killer—"

"What about him?"

"Dead end. Local thug. Long rap sheet, but nothing to connect him to organized crime, anything that might make the case more interesting. As far as it looks, a random thug shot Jen for reasons unknown."

"We know that isn't the truth. What about the plans on the black market? Did you pick up anything?"

"Rumors," Wilson said. "There's buzz about a lot of advanced weapon secrets coming on the black market, for anybody who's interested in collecting them. They aren't for sale."

"What do you mean?"

"I mean," the CIA man continued, "they're made available free of charge. Whoever wants them. Lots of buzz, but nobody's taking it seriously yet."

"Who would make plans for advanced weapons available and not charge for them?" Raven asked.

"It makes it tough to trace the source. Nobody's setting sales appointments. They're allegedly on the dark web, waiting for whoever wants them. The search is in progress. Maybe we can take a few down."

"Very strange."

"What's next for you?" Wilson said.

"See my FBI lady. I should call her and explain why I couldn't make it today."

"Don't push yourself. You need rest, too."

"Thanks, Clark."

"Keep in touch if you need anything."

They hung up. Raven put the phone on silent and stretched out on the bed again. He didn't go back to sleep. His mind buzzed with the new information and he tried to sort it into understandable chunks. And it was nice to lay still in a quiet room for a while.

12

"How long are you planning on staying?" Denosha asked at dinner.

The two men stood at the kitchen counter, holding their plates; who needed civilized eating when you were two bachelors—one recent—trying to get by?

"Maybe another couple of days. I can get a hotel if you want to be alone."

"No, you can stay here," Denosha said. "I might get weird if I'm alone."

"Fair enough."

"Why don't you come with me to the office tomorrow, and I'll show you around. You might get a kick out of the place. There might be—"

"What?"

"A few things we need to talk about. Stuff I can't...you know, tell anybody else."

"If you think I'm the right person."

"You are."

"Are we going back to San Francisco?"

"No, the field office. It's not far from here. It's not the

corporate building. We do all our lab work and research there."

"Your *other* office."

"Right."

"No chauffer this time?" Raven asked.

Denosha laughed. "No prying ears is more like it."

DENOSHA LISTENED to Raven's end of the conversation with Clark Wilson before bed.

Now he knew for certain Raven knew everything. Words like *black market* and *see my FBI lady* made it clear Denosha had to get Raven off the scent.

He hoped his "tour" of the field office did the trick. He had yet to discuss the situation with the Frenchman, but it couldn't wait. He had to lay the groundwork *now* and report later.

He had all the angles worked out. If Raven swallowed the hook, David Denosha would walk away unscathed.

THE DRIVE WAS SHORTER than Raven figured.

They followed 101 North to the Bernal exit, and headed west through South San Jose and into an area of rolling brown hills. The waving grass covering most of the slopes and valleys, Denosha said, never turned green. Brown was its perpetual state. As they traveled further from the urban spread, Denosha pulled over and rolled down the windows. The wind was gentle; birds chirped; no city sounds. Denosha grinned.

"It doesn't get any quieter than this," he said.

"One can get used to it, for sure," Raven said.

Denosha raised the windows and drove forward. The road consisted of two lanes, the blacktop smooth, and the curves sharp. Denosha explained it was the only road in and out of their facility. A private road traveled deeper into the hills to their "blast grounds"—where they tested things—but the private road didn't take anybody anywhere they really wanted to go, like home at the end of the day.

"I bet it gets jammed easily," Raven said.

"In and out, every day, yes," Denosha said. "But we can't get it widened or have another built. The environmentalists have a fit and shit themselves silly over whatever insects live in these hills. We never see any animals or anything worth saving. But goddammit if you try and kill a bug nobody has ever heard of, or cares about, and probably could kill you with a bite anyway."

"Do-gooders forever doing good."

Presently the road straightened and led to the automatic gates dividing the road from a series of buildings. Denosha slowed. The guard at the gate appeared ready to deal with trouble. Raven spotted a Glock pistol on his hip, and the tell-tale outline of an AR-15 rifle hanging on the wall of the guard shack.

The research facility beyond the gate was one main building with four other buildings branching out at perpendicular angles. A parking lot covered one side of the flat ground nestled between the slopes of several brown grass mountains, though Raven supposed they might be referred to as "foothills" at the lower levels. Regardless, the facility was well-hidden from the city they'd passed through, and the overall quiet with the accompanying breeze gave Raven a sense of security he hoped wasn't, ultimately, a false one. Metaphorical snakes lurked under the proverbial rocks, and they were ready to strike.

The guard checked Raven's ID despite Denosha assuring

him he was OK; the guard checked Denosha's ID, too. As they drove through, Denosha said the troops had orders to check IDs regardless of whether they recognized a manager or VIP. Raven expected no less from a high security area, and only complimented Denosha on the guards' training. He thought it was silly to brag about.

Denosha followed an access road to the left, curving around the main building in the center. The structure wasn't anything to marvel at. It was a boring steel-and-glass rectangle with sharp corners reflecting the bright sun. Tinted glass. No identifying signs announced the name of the company.

"No signs?"

"Nope. A lot of private aircraft fly over this area. The less we have to show the world, the better."

"Is your blast range restricted airspace?"

"For sure. But the radius doesn't extend to the building. We test our stuff quite a few miles away."

Denosha parked the car close to the rear entrance in a spot reserved for him. He shut the car off and let out a breath. He turned to Raven.

"There are some people I want you to meet," he said, "and then we'll have a talk, okay?"

"Whatever you say."

Denosha unbuckled his seat belt and exited the car. Raven followed, and trailed behind the big boss as they entered the building.

IN THE LOBBY, Denosha secured a guest pass for Raven. He advised his old pal he'd need an escort at all times as well.

"Even to the toilet?"

"I'll wait out in the hall."

The tour, all Denosha could allow, minus the classified area, began. It was like most offices. A lot of cubicles. But Raven noticed, in a few chases, four or five engineers shared one large cube and work space. Teams on specific tasks, Denosha explained.

Denosha thought fast as he took Raven to one of the branch buildings, where noisy automated robots *clunk clunked* and *whirred* as they assembled portions of long and highly-polished tubes. He figured Raven recognized missile parts when he saw them, but showed no more. It was the payload and guidance gear the company considered secret, so they moved on.

They passed doors in one hallway leading to clean rooms where engineers, decked out in plastic overalls, heads and shoulders covered, performed various tests and hand-fitting of what Denosha only referred to as "critical parts". He appreciated Raven's lack of questions.

Denosha led Raven from one branch building to another. The space between was made up of concrete paths, grass, and a few picnic tables. Two engineers sat at one table going over papers. They didn't notice the boss and his guest walk by.

On the ground floor of the second branch building, Denosha steered Raven through more cubes to a space shared by three people. Two men, one woman.

"I'd like you to meet three of my key people," Denosha said. He stopped in the entrance to the large cube and the three engineers ceased their discussion to acknowledge the boss.

"This is Cliff Graham, Joe Hoover, and Winnie Carver," Denosha said. To the three: "This is Sam Raven. He's our new security consultant."

The three engineers took turns shaking Raven's hand.

Denosha grinned because Raven's face went from curious to confused.

13

RAVEN TRIED TO CONCEAL HIS SURPRISE, BUT KNEW IT SHOWED. *What the hell are you doing, David?*

But he stuck with the role knowing answers were forthcoming. Raven shook hands with each of the engineers and, on instinct, sized them up.

Cliff Graham stood tall and trim over the other two; dark hair, a gold earring on his left ear and gold rings on either hand.

Joe Hoover was short and pudgy and had to set down a Diet Coke to greet Raven. His hand was cold from the chill of the soda can.

Winnie Carver's blue eyes sat behind black-rimmed glasses. Her long curly hair looked unbrushed, and the flower-pattern dress she wore concealed everything beneath. Raven's hand almost crushed her much smaller one. She gave off an overall skin-and-bones vibe.

Raven said, "They must be working on the Venom system, right?" He turned to Denosha to catch his pal's reaction. *One surprise for another, old buddy.*

And Denosha did not disappoint.

His face drained of floor and he stuttered in reply.

"Well, uh, yes, exactly."

Raven addressed the trio. "We hear good things about your work. A lot of people are looking forward to the results."

"We have stiff competition," said Cliff Graham. Raven pegged him as the trio's extrovert. His coworkers remained silent but attentive.

"The same people pulling for you would like to see Lockheed and Grumman take a hit for once," Raven said.

Denosha grabbed Raven's arm and told the engineers they'd be back later. Raven trailed Denosha back to the main building, where they went up a flight of steps to a floor of executive officers. Denosha led Raven into his own and shut the door.

"Nice performance, Sam."

"Well, you did call me a security consultant."

Raven stood in the center of the room and rotated to track Denosha as he circled behind his desk. He twisted open the blinds covering the window. Muted sunlight blasted through the tinted glass.

"Sit."

Raven did. He put his arms on the armrests. Denosha sat, too, and leaned forward on his elbows.

"What did she tell you?" he asked.

"Why only introduce me to those three?" Raven countered.

"I asked you first."

"Jen told me you had a plumbing problem on the Venom project, and it was causing a further strain on your marriage, hence her trip to sort things out, and she asked if I might poke around for you."

"That's all?"

"Yes, David. Of course, what I want to know now is how

her murder and the problem with the Venom missiles tie together. I know you didn't do it, or have it done, so maybe you wanted me to meet your engineers—"

"Shut up. *Christ*, stop talking." Denosha leaned back in the chair, his face a map of anger and frustration. He folded his arms.

Raven let the silence grow between them. Denosha did not look at him. He'd shocked his way into the subject to throw David off; now he wanted to see what he did next.

Then: "Why you, Sam?"

"Been wondering the same thing."

"She expected you to show up here and we'd have a grand reunion? *Bullshit*."

"I can only tell you what she said, David. I didn't get a chance to ask her more."

"How long were you with her?"

"Maybe two hours. We met for a drink. I offered to drive her to the airport the next morning."

"Why didn't you—"

"It was hardly the time earlier. And do you *really* think I wanted to relive the moment?"

"No."

"Now, you tell *me* why you called me a security consultant."

Denosha scoffed. "Because she wasn't wrong. We do have a leak in the Venom project. The plans for the weapons are on the black market already—at least partially. Somebody is trying to stir up interest, from countries who may not have any alliance with the US or NATO. Only four people have access to those plans, and I'm one of them. You just met the other three."

"Uh-huh."

"What do you mean?"

Raven shrugged. "Simply acknowledging what you said."

"Uh-huh."

"What do you want me to do, David?"

"I'd like you to check out the three of them, and see if they're the ones who leaked the plans for the Venom weapons."

"I need to see their files," Raven said. "Look over your background check data. Does the FBI do regular check-ups on your people?"

"When they're assigned to a major project, yes."

"How far back do their records go?"

"Several years. All three have worked for me more than ten years."

"All right. Hand 'em over, and I'll get to work."

"Okay."

"And I'll need a car," Raven said.

"You can drive one of mine, no problem."

"David."

"What?"

"Is there anything else you need to tell me?"

Denosha shook his head.

DENOSHA LET Raven have a Dodge Charger with a big motor; it was the least ridiculous car in his garage. Raven powered the big machine up Highway 101 into San Francisco, where he paid $25 to park in a questionable parking lot near a cluster of office buildings taking up a city block. He didn't go to one of the buildings. He crossed the street instead, a backpack over one shoulder. Entering a small café, Raven found Kayla Blaine sitting in a corner. She faced the entrance and smiled as he joined her. His back was exposed to the front door, but he didn't mind. Kayla knew the drill. She could cover him if any bad guys with guns came through the door. Raven set the backpack at his feet.

"Hello, stranger," she said. She stood to hug him, and he embraced her tightly. She squeezed extra hard.

"I'm glad you could meet me," he said. "You look well."

"And you haven't changed a bit."

Raven wasn't sure about the truth of her words, but he also wasn't going to argue. She could see what she wanted. They separated to sit across from each other.

She looked more than *well*, he had to admit. She retained her fit runner's body, but her low BMI made her appear bony. She still had the sharp jaw and prominent chin. She still wore her dark hair long, and it paired well with her blue eyes. She'd been the only member of her family to go into a law enforcement career; they hadn't liked her joining the cops, and Raven wondered if they'd liked her joining the FBI any better.

"Is Fed life agreeing with you?" he asked.

"It's quieter. We spend a lot of time doing investigative grunt work, dotting Is and crossing Ts and all that, but when we finally make an arrest, it's a good one. There's still too much office politics, but I suppose we can never get away from it. At least my boss isn't a mob stooge this time."

Raven smiled. "It helps."

"If we're going to eat, we need to order at the counter," she said.

"Lead the way, it's on me."

"Are those national secrets in your backpack?" she said, rising. He stood with her, but picked up the pack once again.

"Fate of the world in the balance," he said. They joined the line to the counter. The café was clean but had a lived-in look, the patina of 35 years—a sign out front stated they'd been open since 1987. Ancient times, to Raven; he'd been a young lad then, staying out late with friends to ride bikes and play in the creek near the edge of the neighborhood. Much better times than he found himself in now.

They returned to the table with hot sandwiches, pastrami for both as neither had been able to resist the aroma of the meat. As they ate, Raven explained how he'd once again come to San Francisco. He told her everything Jen Denosha had said, and how his interaction with David was going. He noted the strain during and after the office tour, which Kayla didn't comment on. She wanted to know if the three engineers were a deliberate rabbit trail to throw Raven off the scent.

Raven wasn't sure how to answer. He'd been thinking the same thing, but still had little data to work with. He also had trouble coming to a single conclusion. *Truth takes time*, a mentor had once said, when he had similar trouble finding answers to his first major assignment with the CIA.

Raven opened the backpack and handed Kayla the first file. Cliff Graham, the extrovert of the three engineers. His background contained a lot of detail. Early life, family, career details. He was a recovering gambling addict, and the file noted his continued attendance of meetings and avoidance of anything related to betting. No Vegas trips. No visits to on-line casinos. He was taking his recovery seriously and worked hard at staying away from triggers which might make him relapse.

Joe Hoover, the short and pudgy one with the affection for Diet Coke, had a similarly clean background, but a credit check noted the purchase of a sex doll at one time. Kayla laughed it off—it was one of the least offensive purchase items she'd come across in background checks. It qualified Hoover for sainthood. No criminal record, no nefarious group memberships, no social media posts decrying government policy. Hoover kept to himself, and his known associates were equally benign.

Winnie Carter, the bespectacled petite woman in the flower-print dress, owned several cats. She had an irregular dating life, no suspicious paramours as far as the Feds were concerned, and kept to herself.

Their sandwiches long gone, Raven and Kayla were on their second soda refills as they finished examining each file, reading very detail.

"There's nothing here, Raven," Kayla said. "These three are as boring as watching paint dry."

"It's not impossible they were on their best behavior during these checks," Raven said. "You people aren't following them throughout their lives, right?"

"Despite the accusations of the right wing, no. We only check them out when they work on a government project, or become part of a criminal investigation. They might be hiding things, but nobody hides bad habits so well they don't expose something, somehow, whether they mean to or not."

"What do you suggest we do next?" Raven said.

"What's this we, Raven? You're the new security consultant—what's your first thought?"

"Interviews. Another check. Maybe a little deeper than these files go."

"So, you're the fascist," Kayla said. She grinned.

"What do I need to find before you can step in?"

"I need proof they made copies of the plans and put them on the dark web or however they've been distributed. I need evidence. I need the cat lady meeting with a foreign national and passing the papers under a restaurant table. Get it?"

"Hasn't what I told you qualified as enough to start an official inquiry?" he asked.

"I didn't say I was going back to the office to sit on my ass, Raven. I can poke around a little. I want to find the plans, see if anybody has noticed they were available. May even pay Denosha a visit. What I can't do is go George Orwell on three engineers without more evidence. You may get what we need faster than me."

"Maybe talk to my pal at the CIA."

She raised an eyebrow. "Okay."

"And I'll pass whatever I find to you."

"And become one of my 'confidential informants', okay? That's how we'll do it."

"Be careful."

"I can take care of myself, remember?"

"I do indeed," he said.

They stopped talking and watched each other a moment. They'd shared many close moments during their first encounter; Raven had saved her life from multiple assassins, but she'd viewed him with suspicion until he proved he was on her side. They'd shared one or two physical moments before Raven departed the city to move on to the next fight, wherever he found it. They'd parted quietly and without drama, much as they had reunited. Raven was by no means attempting to rekindle the past; but much like facing Jen again after so many years, he was facing Kayla Blaine again. Not as many years had passed, but powerful emotions pulled at him. She was evidence of a normal relationship forever eluding him—by his own choice—and evidence of somebody he had saved from death. It was no consolation for his failure to save Jen, but at least Kayla Blaine demonstrated he wasn't totally useless.

"Thanks for lunch, Raven. You know how to reach me."

They stood up. He took her arm. "Do you have a few minutes? How about a quick walk? No shop talk."

"I'd like it very much," she said.

They exited the deli together.

14

DENOSHA PACED IN HIS HOME OFFICE, WHERE HE'D FINISHED A series of phone calls with other executives in the company. His board of directors wanted him to take a few days off. He was going to comply, but he wasn't ceasing to work one hundred percent. But before he continued with his real business, he had to reach out to Monique once more.

He held his cell in his right hand but debated making the call. Their last exchange had not gone well, though Denosha had yet to receive any reprimand from the old man. He knew his actions wouldn't be appreciated by the big boss. Certainly, Monique was no fan, either. But they had to understand his emotional state at the time. He didn't see it as an outburst for which there was no excuse.

Finally, he stopped pacing to dial her number. She answered.

"What do you want, David?"

"I should apologize," he said, "for last time."

"You should."

"I am. Consider this—"

"Tell me what you want, David."

"It's Raven," Denosha said. "He's interviewing Graham, Hoover, and Carter. I think we should throw one of them to him, and then he'll stop looking into the matter and go away."

"Are you listening to yourself, David?"

"What?"

"Your plan makes no sense. I have a better one. It's time we killed all four of you."

The line clicked in Denosha's ear.

A chill ran through him as his pulse rate jumped. Was she serious or still upset about the drink in her face? Was it time to come clean with Raven, and have him bring in his FBI contact for a full statement? Monique couldn't do anything rash without talking to the Frenchman first, and getting his permission. Maybe the old man would—

No. *Enough!*

Monique and the old man would find agreement.

He either told Raven the truth or prepared to defend himself.

Or die.

RAVEN AND KAYLA agreed to meet again after Raven completed his three interviews with the engineers.

He started with Joe Hoover first, who entered the small room with his Diet Coke, and looked nervous. Raven only had a clip board and a few pages for notes. He advised Hoover it was a routine interview, nothing to be afraid of. Raven asked probing questions about his work and life and noted the thin layer of sweat on the other man's forehead. Air conditioning blew cold, and Raven wore a light jacket yet still felt a chill. Hoover gave a "no" to Raven's final question:

"Have you exposed or sold any company secrets to third parties?"

He spoke to Graham next, the extrovert trying to tie Raven up in general chat before any serious questions began. Raven deflected and focused on the task. Graham didn't sweat or appear nervous and gave the same benign answers, along with a defiant "no" to the final question.

Raven only judged the two men by body language and voice tone. And his instinct on knowing a liar when he saw one. So far, he thought both Hoover and Graham were lying. Neither spoke with consistent tones, and they shifted in their seats every other answer. The infamous "butt scratch," a nervous reaction of somebody under stress. He wondered what the woman would do.

Winnie Carter entered the room with her hair tied back in a bun, same glasses as before, and a top and jeans combo. The jeans looked faded and on their last threads. Another set of negative answers, but at least she didn't fidget or look nervous. She played dumb, though. *Who, me? No, I'd never.* She only shook her head at the final question.

Raven met up with Kayla again in the evening, and they spoke in her office at the local FBI HQ. Like most offices, the majority of the staff cleared out at 5pm, but a lot of the open desks remained occupied as special agents worked the phones or completed reports. Kayla had a private office off the "bullpen" and shut the door.

Raven explained the results of his interviews, and told Kayla they were all lying, but Winnie Carter lied better than her male counterparts. But how could they give off so many "tells" with him doing the interview, and not when the FBI spoke to them?

Kayla believed she had the answer.

"They weren't doing anything when we talked to them,"

she said. "It was easier to hide. Whatever scheme Denosha is pulling, it happened after the Venom project started."

"What do I tell David?"

"I say tell him what you think, and see what happens. One thing's for sure: my office will be making our presence known after what I found today."

"The leak?"

"I talked to your friend at CIA, and he gave me a few bread crumbs to follow. We've confirmed the blueprints are on the dark web, and life is going to get very interesting for David Denosha shortly."

"He told me it's only him and the three engineers who have access to the files," Raven said.

"He's trying to set up his own people to take the heat off him."

"They'll talk."

"If he doesn't realize that, he's an idiot; what's more likely is his connections will remove the loose ends."

"Maybe it will help."

"That's cold, Raven."

"If they're traitors, I'm not terribly interested in their well-being," Raven said. "And if it forces this Monique woman to expose herself further, it only helps the case."

"Try and find out more about her without getting anybody killed," Kayla said. "We need to do things by the book, and as I recall—"

"I don't know how to read."

Kayla laughed. Raven did, too. It was a light moment they both needed.

She continued, "When you see me around the offices—"

"I don't know you."

"Is Denosha at home?"

"He should be. I'll find out when I get there. I'm still staying in the guest cottage."

"All right. Keep in touch."

Raven grinned at her as he rose from his chair. "Yes, ma'am," he said, turning to the door.

"Hey."

He turned back.

"Be careful, okay? I like having you around. I wish you hadn't left."

He nodded. "Me, too." He left her office and made his way through the bullpen to the elevators. He wanted to look back. He wanted to see her reaction. But he forced himself not to look back, because there was no breaking Rule One. He'd done it once and paid for it; never again.

But, yeah, he wished he had stayed. Wished he *could* stay. He stepped into the elevator car and rode down to the lobby.

15

WINNIE CARTER TURNED HER TEN-YEAR-OLD TOYOTA INTO
the driveway of her Morgan Hill home and climbed out. She
grabbed a small bag of groceries from the passenger seat and
used her key at the front door. The bag contained several
cans of food for her cats. She stopped in the doorway when
her eyes landed on the intruder seated at the couch.

"Monique," Winnie said. "What are you—"

"Shut the door, dear," Monique told her. "The cats will get
out."

"Not if they're hungry." But Winnie closed the door
anyway and didn't bother to turn the lock. One of her cats,
Roofus, sat on Monique's lap, and the French woman
scratched the back of his neck with long nails. Roofus's purr
was audible.

"He's such a nice kitty," Monique said. "It would be a
shame if anything happened to him."

"Why would you say something so horrible?" Winnie put
her hands on her hips. This wasn't Monique's first visit, but
she'd never broken into the house before. Winnie decided
she'd need a better security system. Obviously, what came

with the house wouldn't stop somebody who knew what they were doing.

"We need to talk," Monique said.

"Let's go into the kitchen."

"You have wine?"

"Are we going to need it?" Winnie asked.

"You might. I just want a glass." Monique gave Roofus a nudge and the cat jumped off her lap to run into the kitchen. Winnie followed. Monique trailed after her. Winnie cracked open two cans of food for Roofus and the other gathered cats, then opened a bottle of wine and poured two glasses. They moved to the kitchen table.

"All right," Winnie said, "spill the tea."

"Your boss is setting you up."

"Explains the interview."

"The what?"

"Denosha has somebody named Raven—"

"We know of him."

"Well, he interviewed the three of us today as some sort of background check, and it was David's idea. I don't know *what* he's thinking. If this Raven guy finds out anything—"

"Denosha is playing games," Monique said. "He's already proposed sacrificing one or all of you."

Color drained from Winnie Carter's face. "What did you—"

"I told him to forget it." Monique swallowed some wine, but kept eye contact with Winnie over the rim of her glass.

"I suddenly feel," Winnie said, "like I need a vacation."

"We have everything under control."

"You still haven't told me why you're here."

One of the other cats, a fluffy white one, walked under the kitchen table to brush against Winnie's left ankle. She didn't make a move to grab the feline. The cat meowed. Winnie ignored her.

Monique said, "We need to know when we'll have the next set of plans. Only the first one has been made available."

"With the final changes we're making, maybe another 72 hours. Is that all right?"

"Good enough. Now. Something you may not like—"

"Blame David for everything?"

Monique raised an eyebrow. "You're a mind reader."

"Like my brother always says, get them before they get you."

Monique set her nearly-empty glass on the table and stood. Winnie rose with her.

"Don't do anything more till you hear from me again," Monique said. Winnie followed the French woman to the door and let her out. Closing the door, she felt Roofus and Vivi at her feet once again; this time, she picked up both furry animals and carried them back to the kitchen. Her other cats had spread out in the living room. She wasn't one to talk to her pets, she thought it was silly to do so, but sure wished it was possible to communicate. She needed *somebody* to talk to right now.

—————

"THE ANSWER IS NO, Monique. We aren't waiting 72 hours."

Monique sat in the back seat of her car with her mouth agape. Was the old man insane?

"We *need* the other set of plans," she said.

"There are other ways, my dear."

"I don't understand."

"Because you're not in charge."

Monique's reply caught in her throat.

"It's not worth the risk," the Frenchman continued. "A lot can happen in 72 hours."

"All right."

"I expect the matter will be handled in less than eight hours, actually. Be ready."

"I'm ready," she said. But she sighed with frustration. She'd spent a long time cultivating Denosha and his crew. To end the mission without everything they wanted wasn't her idea of a job well done.

But they hadn't counted on Sam Raven showing up.

RAVEN DIDN'T FEEL like eating with chopsticks.

He spooned his Chinese takeout onto a plate while David fussed with the chopsticks included with the meal. They stood at the kitchen counter once again, because bachelor habits die hard no matter how old you are.

"How did the interviews go?" Denosha said.

Raven didn't want to answer. He wasn't struggling with how to tell David his trio of trusted engineers were lying, but he was too tired to process more data, too tired to find ways to break through David's own force field to learn the truth. All he wanted to do was eat and go to bed.

He told David part of what he was thinking, adding: "How about a meeting first thing tomorrow morning?"

Denosha nodded. "The board wants me to take a few days off, so we can talk here."

Raven said the idea sounded fine. But then his food didn't taste good. He was stalling the inevitable because he didn't want to admit his friend was as guilty as his murdered wife claimed he was. He knew what Denosha was doing. He knew Denosha was setting up the engineers to deflect attention from him.

Raven kept eating. He'd faced more than one betrayal in his life, and he had a hard time facing another. And he'd probably not sleep very well if he spent too much time thinking...

Sometimes he reached a point where he couldn't go forward any longer no matter the stakes or motivation. The bitter-sour taste of life in general and unpleasant tasks in particular made the guts revolt and turned the most dedicated man to a shell of his former self. Raven felt the transformation happen as he stood in the kitchen trying to eat his fried rice. *We used to call it fried lice when we were kids...*

Before life went to hell in more ways than one.

16

RAVEN LAY ON HIS BACK AND STARED AT THE CEILING ABOVE. He hadn't bothered to get into pajamas. He only wanted to think quietly in a dark room until nature took over and lulled him to sleep.

The green glow of his cell phone lit the room. The caller ID displayed Denosha's name. Raven answered.

"What is it?"

"We got incoming, Sam! Get over here!"

Raven rolled off the bed and grabbed his shoulder rig from the nightstand. Slinging his arms through the harness with its two spare magazines, he drew the .45 and ran outside.

He almost didn't make it out the door.

Raven stopped short; so did a gunman dressed in black, his face covered with streaks of camouflage paint. He held a suppressor-fitted M-4 carbine. The M-4 and Raven's pistol came up at the same time, but Raven fired first. The triple-tap of .45 ACP hollow-points made a triangle of fleshy red punctures on the gunman's face. The impacts accomplished the desired effect. The gunman dropped, Raven squatting beside him, jamming the .45 back under his arm. He helped himself to the M-4 and noted the extra magazine taped to the bottom of the first for a quick reload.

A shotgun blast broke through the ringing in Raven's ears. He looked at the front gate; it had been breached, both sides open to allow access. Had they known about the laser alarm, they might not have bothered, and Raven hoped the warning gave him and David the edge. The killers were down one man, but how many more did they have?

The area around the house looked clear. Another shotgun blast suggested all the action was inside. Raven decided he needed to be there, too.

He ran, but not for the front door. He ran for the back patio. The sliding glass doors to the kitchen served as his entry point, and he scooped up a chair with his free left hand. He flung the chair into the glass. The pane shattered with a loud crash and glass spilled out onto the patio and interior carpet. Bits of glass fell down the back of his shirt as he ran through the hole, but he didn't have time to fuss. A third shotgun blast boomed. David was holding his own. All Raven had to do was avoid any friendly fire.

"David!" Raven raced through the first floor, checking rooms and corners; no gunmen. Denosha's strained reply came from upstairs.

And now the enemy knew they faced more than one target. Raven may have given up the element of surprise, but he'd also taken the heat off David. The enemy had to divert one or two to deal with the new arrival who was supposed to be already dead.

Raven reached the front of the house and eased up the wide, curving staircase with his back to the wall.

"How many, David?"

No reply. No more shotgun blasts, either. Raven tucked

the M-4 into his shoulder and let the muzzle probe the second-floor landing and the mouth of the dark hallway. He wished David had given him a tour of the place. They'd had other things on their minds. He had no idea what was on the second floor. He'd have to improvise. Wouldn't be the first time.

A shadow moved against the dark hallway. Raven almost hesitated to fire, but a small flash of white skin streaked with black proved he wasn't firing on David. Raven let the captured M-4 talk. Two rapid blasts of suppressed 5.56mm tumblers smacked into the shooter's chest. He didn't fall— body armor. The gunman grunted and started to move back. Raven adjusted his aim and pulled the trigger again. The shot cored the killer's skull. The gunman fired into the ceiling as he fell to the carpet.

Raven advanced two more steps. His pulse hammered. Sweat trickled down the side of his face. *Where's David?* Another step up...

A line of slugs chewed into the wall. Raven dropped but landed awkwardly on the steps. One of his feet slipped. He tumbled down the staircase as more rounds tore the wall to pieces. Bits of sheetrock and molding rained on Raven as he tumbled. He stopped hard on the tiled floor at the foot of the stairs. The gunman above strayed in the darkened hallway. Raven heard the *click-clack* of changing magazines. He rolled away from the staircase, jerking his head around to find cover. There was none. He was exposed in the middle of the entryway.

Raven came to a rest on his back, switched the M-4 to full-auto, and let the gunman have a long burst. He wasn't going for a kill shot, though it would have been nice; instead, he wanted to drive the gunman to cover and buy time. As he jumped to his feet and ran for a doorway, a chill rushed through him. David not arriving with his shotgun meant one thing. He wasn't alive any longer to help Raven finish the fight.

Raven flipped magazines, slamming home the full mag attached to the empty. Boots pounded down the steps. The top portion of the staircase was cut off by the hallway ceiling over the doorway, but Raven didn't rush. With the M-4 at the ready, he waited. The gunman fired probing shots; none connected. When the killer's legs appeared in view midway, Raven fired. The gunman's knees weren't protected. The 5.56mm slugs popped the killer's left knee like an egg cracked on the edge of a skillet. The gunner cried out as he fell down the steps, losing his grip on the M-4, sprawling onto the tile. He struggled to rise. Raven walked over and shot him in the back of the head. He stepped over the body and took the steps two at a time.

"David!"

Raven found him at the end of the hall, flat on the floor of his office. The shotgun lay beside him. Holes from multiple rounds had ripped open his chest, and the mess of bloody flesh turned inside out froze Raven in place. All feeling departed his body; replaced by despair. First Jen; now David. And Raven had no idea *why*.

He wasn't going to wait for cops. He knew who the enemy was; knew how to find her. He had to work fast.

Grabbing his wallet and phone from the cottage, stuffing clothes back into his suitcase, he ran to the attached garage. He still had the keys to David's Dodge. Climbing into the car as the automatic garage door opened, he started the engine. Raven plowed through the half-open gate and onto the access road. He wiped sweat from his face; the windows were down, cold air rushing in, but he was still flush with heat.

He had to get to Kayla's. They'd access David's "cloud" storage and get a positive ID on the woman who had visited.

They'd find a way to get the engineers to—Raven stopped his train of thought.

He wasn't certain the three engineers were still alive.

The next step started with Monique and nobody else.

If she hadn't fled the country.

17

RAVEN PHONED KAYLA BLAINE ON THE WAY. HE FOLLOWED Highway 101 into the city and exited the freeway at King Street. He found his way to the Embarcadero and turned right. Her condo in the Rincon Tower wasn't far. He had to park on the street but ignored the meter. For now.

When she answered the door, Kayla let out a sharp gasp and covered her mouth.

"Are you hurt?"

"Let me in," Raven said, stepping past her into the condo. She shut the door and set the locks. She turned to him.

"What happened, Raven?"

He let out a breath of his own and asked where he might put his suitcases.

"Just leave them there. Go sit down. I'll get you a drink."

"Anything with alcohol," he told her. He set down the suitcases and made his way to the couch. Kayla fussed in the kitchen. Ice clinked into glasses.

Raven rubbed his face and wiped his hands on his jeans. His hands shook. Shock coming on. He didn't see Kayla return. She had to say his name to get his attention. He took the glass she offered. Bourbon over ice. Exactly what he needed. Kayla sat next to him but not too close.

He glanced at her. Her face looked plain without makeup, a look he'd seen before, and found more appealing than when it was the opposite. She wore sweat pants and a tank top. Her bare feet were tipped with red toenails.

"Denosha?" she said.

Raven swallowed a mouthful of bourbon and related the story. Kayla listened without comment until he finished, and then Raven filled the silence by taking another drink. The ice cubes clinked together. He set the glass on the coffee table in front of him.

"Refill?"

Raven shook his head.

"We'll deal with the police in the morning," she said.

"I need a shower."

"Of course. I'll get a towel for you."

"Can your office get into Denosha's cloud storage?"

"You can do anything with a court order in a case involving national security."

She set out a towel and showed him how to work the shower and left him alone. Raven was sore and grimy all over. It felt good to get out of his clothes and under the hot spray. He set his locket carefully on the bathroom counter. He leaned against the wall, letting the hot water beat against him, the steam filling the stall, coating the glass doors. He wondered what he might have done differently to save David's life. There were still so many unanswered questions, he wasn't sure where to start.

He took the soap from the holder.

The sliding glass door opened behind him. "I'll take that," Kayla said.

Naked, she stepped into the shower and took the soap from his hands.

RAVEN GUESSED CORRECTLY. All three engineers on the Venom project met violent ends the night before, in their homes; they'd even shot Winnie Carver's cats. Kayla accessed the information on her laptop while they ate breakfast.

Raven's thoughts were scattered and anxious. He wasn't quite near a panic attack, but certainly close. The events since Jen's murder, culminating with David's murder and the attack on the house, left him reeling. The war without end was taking a toll, and he needed more than the temporary reprieve with Kayla to take his mind off the situation.

There was only one way to solve the problem. Find the truth. Punish the guilty. Avenge his friends. Because, no matter what, David Denosha had been a friend once. Whatever he'd done had more than likely spiraled out of any sort of control long before the enemy sent a gunman to kill Jen.

He and Kayla ate quietly while discussing the new information, and what they needed to go over at Kayla's office. Kayla called ahead to make sure her support crew had details ready for their arrival, and she especially wanted to know what the cops had found. Raven remained quiet as she thought out loud. He wanted to know, too, but didn't see much point in getting too deep in the weeds. They needed to look for Monique. She was his only concern as he washed down the eggs and toast with a last gulp of hot tea.

Raven wore jeans and a button-down shirt to the FBI office. He looked out of place with Kayla and the other agents in their formal attire.

The window of Kayla's office overlooked the city, and part of the bay, but Raven's focus was on the dossier on her computer screen. They sat next to each other behind her desk, with Kayla manipulating the mouse to display different pages and photos.

"Told you we'd pull the cloud footage," she said. "This is the night you arrived and saw your mystery woman."

The color footage showed the woman's arrival. Kayla paused the picture and typed a command. The picture grew in size. Raven leaned close. The woman's features weren't as sharp as he'd have liked, but he saw enough.

"Can you get an ID based on this image?" he asked.

She typed another command. "Already have."

The video capture vanished in favor of a criminal advisory from Interpol. The text was in French, but a corner photo showed a mugshot of the woman. She lacked makeup and didn't look as good as in the video, but there was no mistake. Same full lips, dark eyes, long black hair. Kayla typed another command and the text changed to English.

"Monique Choffron," Kayla said. "Spent her life in the underground. Her father was a French mob boss. He was killed when she was in her 20s, and she drifted onto the streets for a few years."

"Who killed her father?"

"She's actually the prime suspect."

"Nice girl," Raven said. He read more of the file.

"This mugshot," Kayla said, "was taken after a human trafficking arrest, but she beat the charge."

"They usually do." Raven sat back. "Known associates?"

Another click; another dossier page. "We have a few," Kayla said.

Raven read the list of names. "Most of these guys are dead."

"Should narrow it down, right?"

"What I'd like to know is where she might be right now."

"The Bay Area is a big place; she might be anywhere."

"She'll be close. I have a feeling."

"I'll put the crew on it. Might take a while."

While her team of agents searched, she and Raven began

hunting through Monique's known aliases. Perhaps she was using one; a combination of others; or, if they were lucky, her own name. She wasn't currently wanted by any police agency, in the United States or around the world. After her trafficking arrest, she had very little recorded activity. Raven found the fact of interest. She might have been working for somebody else, a figurehead who pulled the strings. Were there others like David? If Raven could find them and assemble a pattern of movement, the trail might lead to her. Anyway, it was an idea. And without a solid lead, he needed all the ideas he could bring to mind.

The search for aliases scored a hit. Monique Choffron lived in Daly City under the name Stephanie Vamos, a combination of two earlier aliases used in Paris.

"Let's go see if we can borrow a cup of sugar," Kayla said.

18

KAYLA DROVE. SHE FOLLOWED HIGHWAY 280 SOUTHBOUND out of San Francisco. It was not a long drive to Daly City, and when she pulled off the freeway, Kayla followed a series of blocks and a few turns to a condo complex. Lots of white stucco and tan tiled roofs made up the complex. The only way to tell them apart were outside displays, and there were only a few of those, because residents probably had to deal with a Nazi-like homeowner's association. Such associations were the last vestiges of the Third Reich, Raven believed.

When they reached the unit "owned" by Ms. Vamos, they stopped before the door. The door was open a crack. Raven took out his gun while Kayla pushed the door open. Raven entered first as she drew her own weapon.

"FBI!" Kayla shouted. "Anybody—"

Raven held up a hand. Kayla didn't finish her question. The place was furnished, but devoid of life. They checked the rooms. No dead bodies. No clothes or other personal items in the bedroom or elsewhere. Monique Choffron had cleared out and left little of value behind. She hadn't even bothered to close the front door when she departed. Still, they searched. Just in case. The search didn't take long and they were back on the road returning to San Francisco.

"She bailed," Raven said.

"Lived up to her alias." Kayla cracked a smile. "But she forgot this." She pulled a folded picture from the pocket of her blazer. She passed the picture to Raven.

"Who is this?" It was a picture of Monique and another man. He had shaggy hair and glasses. They posed in front of a swimming pool. Monique wore a bikini showing every curve she had, while her male companion displayed a ripped physique only a gym rat achieved.

"We'll find out," she said. "It was in a frame that fell behind the empty shelf in the living room."

Raven examined the photo trying to find the man's face in his mental mug file, but no dice. He hoped Kayla and her team of Feds had better luck.

THE MAN in the picture turned up as Ramon Crozier, a night club owner in Paris with no criminal record. But the police suspected him of being connected with the same unsavory characters Monique Choffron grew up with; there was a note his club might be used for money laundering, but no evidence.

"I hope they haven't broken up," Kayla said later, as she and Raven ate lunch in a busy park behind the Metreon Center. The shopping center contained more than one restaurant; opposite the park, there were museums and other places to get lost for an afternoon. They sat on the grass under a tree.

Raven ate some of his corned beef. "Chance I'll take."

"I wish I could ask you to stay," she said.

"I know," he said.

"What if I asked you to come back? When it's over. For a few days."

Raven didn't want to make such a commitment. He told himself it was because he might not make it back, but it wasn't true. He was usually smart enough not to lie to himself. If he came back, he might not want to leave. But he had his rule for a reason. He couldn't stay long, but it didn't mean he couldn't find a temporary respite from his war without end.

"I can come back," he said, "for a few days."

"That would be nice."

He thought so, too.

MONIQUE CHOFFRON LEFT San Francisco under her false name and hoped it was enough protection to get her back home. The hit team didn't connect to her, but she wanted a clear trail in case any investigation turned up her name one way or another. US authorities worked slowly. First, they'd connect the murders. Then they'd see who the victims had in common. Maybe one of the engineers wrote a diary; they'd find her name eventually. The goal was to be long gone before they did. She had time to escape, but not if they found a record of her departure under her real name.

There were far too many places to hide where US agents could never find her. And Monique had grown accustomed to changing her name as often as she washed her hair.

She sat in first class and rested her head on a neck pillow. Noise-cancelling headphones covered her ears. Three screaming babies rode on the plane, albeit well behind her, but their cries were audible without the headphones. She refused to let their screaming terrorize her.

Monique was on her way to Paris. It wasn't her first

choice of locations to run to. It was home. She lived there. But the boss had called a meeting. She had to give the Source an update on events in San Francisco. She was sure the Frenchman had new orders for her as well. The flight across the ocean would be all the rest she'd get before the next job. The Source did not rest; the Frenchman did not want his people idle. The fate of the world depended on their adeptness from one task to the next.

The Frenchman's goals were not within Monique's usual area of expertise. But her skills at subversion made the accomplishment of the goals much easier. He hired people like her—career criminals—to carry out his vision. She dozed off with the thought she'd always have a job as long as she stayed with the Source. Their work would never reach completion. She wondered if the Frenchman realized he wouldn't live long enough to see his vision's fruition.

She wasn't going to tell him, however. No, sir. Not as long as she liked getting paid. The Frenchman spared no expense and allowed Monique to maintain her high-living lifestyle. She'd come a long way from her father's shadow. She'd earned every penny.

19

A CHATEAU OUTSIDE PARIS. HIDDEN WITHIN GREEN TREES, walled off from the outside. The meeting assembled on the lower floor in a large room of shiny wood flooring and stone walls. Three rows of chairs faced a dais. As the attendees waited, they chattered about an empty chair in the first row. Monique Choffron was late. Then all eyes turned to a door off to their left. Monique entered with a stoic expression and casual step. The chatter stopped. She zeroed on the empty chair in the front row and sat without acknowledging any of her colleagues.

Monique sensed their eyes on her; she gave them no reaction. They wanted to know what happened in California. She wasn't interested in talking until necessary, until the old man asked for her presentation. The others could wait until then.

A hush fell over the room as a door behind the dais opened and closed. The old man entered. He wore a conservative grey suit, his hair white, the lines on his face suggesting more than his 70 years. He was a man who had seen a lot of war and violence, and he wanted to put an end to war in his lifetime. It was a strange goal, but he went about his dream with the dedication of a religious zealot. The goal was every-thing. Nothing, and nobody, could stand in the way. Monique thought he was stupid. Humans liked war. History proved time and again it was the only thing they, as a species, excelled at. To her mind, there was more profit in selling the tools of war. Why not take advantage of the situation? But the Frenchman had other ideas. And, in a way, he had adopted some of Monique's attitude.

They called him the Frenchman. His real name was Pierre Broularid, known throughout the world as a giant of banking and finance. He made his fortune early in life, and spent his later years growing richer with each passing stock trade or company sale. Monique liked how her job never ran short of money, or what she needed to pay off opposition. Or pay for a team of expert killers to *remove* opposition.

But she was nervous as Broularid took his seat on the dais and faced them. After a slow examination of each face, he called the meeting to order. His deep, low voice filled the room.

"We have many matters to discuss, but foremost on my mind is the problem with Denosha Defense in the United States. Monique, I want to know what happened. In *detail*. Why do we find ourselves in our present difficulties?"

Monique frowned. She didn't understand. The problem was solved!

She swallowed and cursed her dry throat. The Frenchman didn't allow drinks in meetings. He stared at her. His eyes showed severe disapproval. It was the same look her father had once given her moments before she fired bullets into his body.

She stood from her chair and approached Broularid. She faced the gathering.

"I've spent the last two years in San Francisco with Denosha Defense. In that time, we collected a great deal of classified information on new missile systems. The CEO, David Denosha, was simpatico with our cause, and a willing participant. His wife was also on board, until she wasn't. She began plotting to expose our operation and decided to run. We kept close watch on her. On her way to Barbados, she stopped in Washington, DC, and met with a man named Sam Raven..."

She explained the rest of the story. She concluded with the hit team killing Denosha and Raven. And how she *personally* dispatched the three engineers also involved in the conspiracy.

Monique turned to the Frenchman. "I don't understand why you call my efforts a problem. It was a success."

"You failed."

Her mouth opened to respond but no words came out.

"Sit down."

She straightened, pivoted, and returned to her seat with her jaw clenched tight.

"Sam Raven is still alive," Broularid said.

Finally, Monique found her voice.

"How?" she shouted.

"Control yourself. David Denosha is dead; Sam Raven is not. Our problem is not solved, it has multiplied. We must alert our people to be aware of him, and on the lookout for anybody he may recruit to interfere with our plans. World peace depends on us. I do not care how many we have to kill to achieve our goal; there will be no more war. *None!*"

If the words had come from anybody else, Monique might have laughed. But Broularid's dichotomy no longer confused her. She didn't bother to try and figure him out. His vision called for a different extremism; a new kind of jihad.

Monique took a deep breath to settle her nerves. She wanted to be in charge of the hunt for Sam Raven. As soon as she had the opportunity, she wanted to further research his life. She wanted to discover what kind of man she was dealing with. The more she knew, the easier it would be to kill him. She'd need the best to deal with him, and the best wouldn't come cheap. Broularid already knew that particular truth. He'd never failed to provide what she needed before; he wouldn't let her down now. Not when his dream was under attack. It was as much his neck on the line as hers at this point.

———————————

SHE NEEDED A BREAK.

But Monique also required her boyfriend's input on Sam Raven. The Frenchman hadn't yet said anything about her going after Raven, or arranging such, but she was determined to finish the job.

She paid off her taxi and stepped onto the sidewalk in front of Ramon's nightclub, the name of which was a play on his last name. The Cozy Club had become one of the premier nightspots in Paris thanks to Ramon's management. The club was closed till evening, but she knocked a tap code on the door to let Ramon know it was her.

Ramon Crozier answered the door and smiled. "You're here, finally," he said. He pushed open the door and her heels clicked as she moved past him. He shut the door and turned the lock.

Two years since they'd last seen each other, and they crushed one another in their arms and kissed long and hard. By the time she pulled back, she was out of breath.

Nightclub interiors always made Monique pause. They were a different place with the lights on and chairs stacked. The polished floor reflected much of the overhead light; Ramon stepped in front of her with his arms out.

He made a turn and said, "What do you think? New floor, cleaned up the bar, look at how much bigger the stage is!"

Monique folded her arms and gave the place a cursory look. She nodded in appreciation. "Very good, honey. I like it."

Frankly, the changes didn't mean much. She visited the club so little he could have moved to another location and the change might have escaped her notice, too.

Monique and Ramon Crozier had an on again, off again, mostly on relationship, but she wasn't sure how serious they were. They were serious enough not to stray, but had long ago accepted they each stayed busy with their respective business activities and saw each other when time allowed. It worked for them.

"Are you even paying attention?" Ramon asked. He wore dark clothes, but left his shirt unbuttoned enough to show the white skin underneath. As a night owl, his skin looked pale; the patch of white clashed with the dark outfit.

"It's wonderful, darling. I can see you've been working hard."

"And you?" He approached her and they kissed again briefly; she pulled back first.

"I need your help on something," she said. "We need to do a little research. I have a mistake to correct."

"Who are you trying to kill?"

The Cozy Club served as a front. Ramon's side business included gathering stray information relating to Western intelligence and selling it to interested parties. His clients usually weren't allies of the west.

The Source had access to the underground data stream where she might find Sam Raven's secrets, but then the Frenchman would look over her shoulder. She wanted to deliver the information on her own. It would show initiative.

She had a feeling the Frenchman wasn't happy with her despite not saying so specifically.

"Let's go to my office," he said.

She followed him up a set of stairs off the polished dance-floor. Ramon's office occupied a second-level platform over the stage, with a rail and walkway in front of the door to allow him to survey the nightly activity. He unlocked his office and entered first to flip on a light.

Desk on the left, sitting area to the right; the thin carpet appeared loose at the edges. Ramon's upgrades had not reached his own work space yet.

Ramon dropped into the chair behind his desk while Monique sat in front. She crossed her legs. He booted his desktop.

"Who are we looking for?"

"A man named Sam Raven."

He cocked an eyebrow at her.

"Are you kidding?"

"Do you know him?"

"I know *of* him. I know enough to stay away from *anywhere* he might be."

"What's his story?"

"You don't know?"

"I've been a little busy, hon."

"He's a crusader. He doesn't tolerate…people like *us*."

"There has to be a way to find him. He has friends somewhere."

Ramon began typing, and when the details of Raven's available background appeared on the screen, he rotated the monitor so she had a better view.

"We know he's American, special ops background. Why he began his vigilante activity, nobody knows," Ramon said.

"He magically appeared."

"Something pissed him off. He's killed a ton of people he's

deemed in need of killing. Thinks of himself as a sort of protector, savior of victims, that sort of thing."

"Uh-huh. Tell me something I can use. How do I get to him?" Monique asked.

"Why the interest?"

She told him about the Denosha assignment, and the clean-up involving the kill team.

Ramon cracked a grin. "You had a friend of his murdered? Be patient. He'll come to *you.*"

"Idiot. This is why I need leverage. Nobody's invincible."

Ramon turned the monitor back to him and consulted the screen, scrolling through the displayed information.

"He has a CIA contact, a man named Clark Wilson." He turned the monitor to her again. She leaned closer to read the name.

"Where do I find this man?"

"He lives in the US. Probably somewhere in Virginia."

"Find out. I have another call to make."

20

His name was Callen Cord and he lived by his own set of rules: whoever has money, makes the rules.

Once a highly-decorated CIA officer, he now worked freelance, often for Western intelligence agencies but now and then for less savory types; his government employers let him mix with certain undesirables because he often brought back useful information on third parties the West has an interest in learning more about. His duplicity was a carefully guarded element to his line of work. Should those he betrayed ever learn about what he did, they'd cut his throat.

Cord sat outside a small café in DC, sipping his brew and looking up sports scores on his phone. When a text chimed with only three words—"Client for you"—he plugged a Blue-tooth into his right ear and called home base where a woman named Caroline answered.

"You got a job if you want it," Caroline said. She was one of two intermediaries he used to screen customers.

"Tell me about it."

"She's from France, gave only her first name, and wants to talk to you about a surveillance job here in DC."

"Cute."

"She didn't tell me more, but she's willing to add ten percent to your usual fee. She says you've worked for her before."

"Name?"

"Monique."

"Oh, *her*. Okay. I'll call back after I'm done with my coffee."

"I'll forward her contact number."

"Thank you, Caroline."

"No problem, chief."

She disconnected and Cord put the Bluetooth away and returned to his sports scores and coffee. He blended well with the other people around him. He was in better shape than most, but hid the fact by sitting with a slight slouch. His table was close to the hard wall of the café, so he might see anybody coming at him from the front, and his windbreaker was half-zipped to conceal the Smith & Wesson pistol under his left arm. Shaggy haircut, three-day beard; he was everyman and no man at the same time.

Later, in the safe confines of his car, he dialed the number Caroline forwarded and waited for Monique to answer.

"Hello?" She sounded tired. Cord figured he woke her as it was nighttime in Paris.

"It's Cord. You called."

The woman's voice brightened. "Yes. Are you available?"

"For ten percent over, yes."

"It's an easy job."

"Let's hear it."

She told him.

Cord accepted the job and asked Monique to put half the money in his account and the other half on completion. She agreed.

Cord ended the call and set his phone on the passenger

seat. He grabbed another phone from the glove box and dialed a second number.

"This is Clark," the man on the other end answered.

"It's Cord."

"Hey!" said Clark Wilson at his office in CIA headquarters. "Been a while. How are you?"

"Very well. But I have a problem."

"What's your trouble?"

"Somebody wants me to spy on you."

"Tell me more..."

———

CLARK WILSON HUNG up after his conversation with Callen Cord and pressed his lips together. He needed to call Raven right away; he was reaching for the phone when it rang again. He picked up. "This is Clark."

"It's Sam."

Clark Wilson eased back in his chair. "I was about to call you. Get this. Some lady in Paris has hired a freelancer to find *you* through *me*."

"Named Monique?"

"How did you guess?"

"I've been busy in San Francisco, Clark. I'll fill you in, then tell me your side."

Wilson listened while Raven related the story of the past few days, culminating with the murders of Denosha and his engineers, and the quick exit of Monique Choffron from Daly City.

"I'm leaving for Paris next flight," Raven said. "I'm going to check out her boyfriend. Now tell me yours."

"She's looking for you," Wilson said. "Her info must be solid because she somehow picked out our connections and thinks I'm the best way to find you."

Wilson explained his conversation with Cord.

"Who is this fellow?" Raven asked.

"You'd like him. Former officer, like you, very handy with wet work and all that. He does jobs for us and the Brits and Mossad, but now and then he works for the ungodly, but manages to tell us a thing or two if he picks up information he thinks we'll like. He's never done any job to hurt the US or our allies. He's solid, Sam. Doesn't talk much but you can trust him."

"It seems to me this is an opportunity we shouldn't pass up."

"I agree. But it has to look good."

"Certainly," Raven said. "I'd hate for Mr. Cord to not earn his fee. You two going to meet?"

"In a few hours, yeah. I'll advise him of our chat and we can go from there."

"All right. Are the cops still asking about me?"

"Your FBI friend has made enough noise to get the heat off. Don't worry about Metro. They're off the case."

"Okay."

"Sam?"

"Yeah."

"I'm sorry about Denosha."

"Not as sorry as that bitch is going to be when I catch up with her."

Kayla Blaine pulled up to the curbside check-in outside the SFO terminal and gave Raven a sad glance.

"Do we say good-bye?"

Raven unlatched his seat belt. "I keep my promises," he said. "This is only a detour."

"Be careful, Raven."

He leaned over and kissed her. The move startled her; by the time she began to kiss back, he pulled away. He must have seen the shock on her face because he only grinned and then opened the passenger door and stepped out. She watched him grab his luggage from the back seat and turn away. He didn't look back.

Kayla laughed to herself, put the car in gear, checked to make sure it was safe to pull away, and accelerated from the terminal.

I keep my promises.

But she knew Raven and knew his life and hoped he lived to indeed return. As he promised.

21

RAVEN SETTLED BACK IN HIS FIRST-CLASS SEAT AS THE JETLINER left the tarmac and climbed over the bay waters. He'd have preferred his private jet and his own flight crew, but there was no time to wait for them. They'd have had to come across the ocean to collect him. A commercial jet was the most efficient way to get to Paris, and he traveled under his own name. He wasn't worried about the enemy finding him. If they did, so much the better—he wouldn't have to find *them*.

He wondered about the freelancer named Callen Cord and how they might work out the arrangement required to make Cord's job look good. It was a dangerous ploy. The other side might discover the ruse; they might not. They wanted Cord to find him so they could kill him, but at least he'd know they were coming. He needed every edge available. He wanted the enemy to hurt the way he hurt. He wanted to know the truth about why Jen and David died, even when the truth revealed the extent of his late friends' involvement with the other side.

He felt for the locket under his shirt. The ghosts of his

past were going ahead of him, as always; guiding him through the war without end.

And there was no end. He was a fool to think otherwise.

Some people lived their lives wondering what their purpose on earth might be.

But Raven knew *his*.

It was time to stop running from his purpose and embrace it once again.

The recent months had been hard, the fighting fierce, and too many had fallen whom Raven had tried to protect. The toll taken was more than he expected, but the way wasn't going to stop. No amount of wishing could change what he had to do, what he was *called* to do by forces he didn't understand. It was time to channel the rage, the pain, and desire for peace into the fight. The enemy had to pay for every drop of blood spilled.

It was the only way to break the cycle. Bring the pain to the enemy *first*.

As long as he drew breath.

———

As CLANDESTINE MEETINGS WENT, Clark Wilson and Callen Cord didn't play games.

Assume they're watching.

And whoever this Monique person was, Clark figured, she might indeed have Cord under watch, so their connection had to look good. They wanted to show she was getting what she paid for.

Wilson called his wife and told her he'd miss dinner, but he also wouldn't be out late. He didn't expect his chat with Cord to last more than an hour. He took a table at a restaurant in downtown Langley and sipped ice water while consulting the menu. When Cord joined him, he glanced over the edge of the menu and greeted his old friend with a handshake.

"Would it kill you to get a haircut?" Wilson said.

Cord scoffed. "Nice thing about working for yourself. You should try it."

"I got a kid in college."

"Which one?"

"My daughter," Wilson said. "My son is a senior. Graduates in a few months."

"Then you'll have *two* in college."

"Which means no privateering for me," Wilson said. "Well, I never thought they'd get out of diapers let alone university."

"Uh-huh."

"Get whatever you want," Wilson said as the waitress brought Cord's menu. He ordered a vodka tonic. "It's on Uncle Sugar," Wilson added.

"Nice to get something out of the old bastard for a change," Cord said.

Wilson had removed his tie and loosened the top buttons on his dress shirt, but he still appeared overdressed compared to Cord's T-shirt and jeans. He wondered if the freelancer packed any weapons. He didn't see how Cord could hide his usual hardware. Then again, he realized, Raven was the only one he knew who never went out unarmed.

"How's life been treating you?" Wilson said.

They caught up and made small talk about sports; after placing their orders and another round of drinks, Wilson finally brought up the reason for their meeting.

"What's your plan?"

Cord shrugged and sipped his drink. "I was thinking of cloning your cell phone, and tracing any calls from Raven."

"Not too shabby. I've spoken to Sam about you, and he's

down for whatever we come up with. They ask you to do anything other than find him?"

Cord shook his head. "Not yet."

"Then let's let them dangle a bit. He's on his way to them, so between the three of us we can accelerate this caper and bring it to a close."

"Any idea what it's all about?"

"Not yet, but here's what I have so far…"

They continued the conversation as they ate, and finally Cord offered an opinion.

"Making designs available at no cost? Very strange. There's something more going on."

"I'm going to try and find other David Denoshas who may have passed secrets. This group, whoever they are, is far to organized for Denosha Defense to be their only effort so far."

"What do I tell them about Raven?"

"Tell them he's in Paris."

Monique was too nervous to sit.

The Frenchman had summoned her. For what, she did not know. At least she had something to report, a nugget to let him know she hadn't failed completely. She had a way to find Sam Raven. If this was the kiss off, if he wanted to see her privately to deal with her supposed failure, perhaps her nugget would earn a stay of execution.

Monique didn't view the San Francisco effort as a disaster. Sure, one target escaped the kill squad, but what did Raven know? *Nothing.* Denosha had been stringing him along, feeding him whatever story was convenient, making him believe the three engineers were the guilty party. Anything to keep his pal from discovering the truth. Raven had more questions than answers and the only people who might reveal details were cold in the morgue.

In a perfect world, Raven would be on ice, too. But the world wasn't perfect. With a little effort, one might make it *almost* perfect, and Monique had to make her boss see she had done everything in her power to keep the advantage they'd so far enjoyed. She had to make him realize his vision was not in danger.

She paced the room. She was in a small library somewhere in the chateau, and she had to avoid banging into the leather couches forming a square in the center of the room with the glass coffee table in the bull's eye. The books lining the walls covered a wide variety of subjects, and the Frenchman had then arranged and grouped the books by topic. Most were history-related; others biographies of the military greats; still more politically-focused. All appeared read based on the creases in the spines, and none had been read only once.

The door behind her opened and clicked closed. Monique turned around.

Pierre Broularid, the Frenchman, didn't smile. He wore a brown sweater and tan slacks. He looked like somebody's grandfather, Mr. Rogers between seasons, and Monique supposed he might be. She had no idea if he had a family, and he'd never volunteered the information.

"Were you not offered a drink?" he asked.

"I refused."

"Change your mind? I'm having one?"

Broularid crossed to a corner bar and lifted the stopper from a crystal decanter. He filled a glass with an amber liquid. "You sure?"

"Fine."

He poured another and brought her the glass. She

accepted it and sipped the warm bourbon; it fell hard in her belly. She was in no state to enjoy anything.

"I have something to show you," Broularid told her. He went to a desk in another corner and opened a drawer. She watched him remove a tablet computer; he closed the drawer.

She said, "I have somebody looking for Sam Raven."

"I know."

"What—"

"It doesn't matter. I *know*. It is my business to know what my people are doing. Do not be upset with Ramon. He is not my source."

He handed her the tablet and she took it with her free hand without thinking. The display showed a familiar pattern, and she examined the screen with curious eyes. Moving to one of the leather sofas at the center of the room, she scrolled through several pictures, noting the line drawings and technical notes.

"This is—"

"The remaining plans for the Denosha Venom project." He sat on the couch opposite her. "We had 72 hours, remember?"

She raised an eyebrow. Monique did not look happy.

"Always have a backup, Monique. It's the one thing you haven't learned."

"You had another—"

He raised a hand. "Yes. I only called him as it was an emergency. If you had completed the task, I'd have not have bothered my other source."

"Are you trying to make me foolish?"

The Frenchman sighed and swallowed more of his drink. He sat back and crossed his legs.

"What did you expect when you came here, Monique? Hmmm?"

Her hard expression gave no clue to her thoughts.

"You expected punishment? I was going to feed you to sharks? I have no sharks, Monique. I don't have a dungeon, either. I am not what you think I am." He paused a moment, then: "I'm not your father."

She flinched.

"What I *am* trying to do is protect an investment. You've done well overall. The Denosha problem we can attribute to a variable element for which there was no immediate solution."

"Okay."

"But we must *discover* a solution and do so with great haste. Which is why I'm pleased you took steps to find Mr. Sam Raven."

Monique took a drink. It tasted better now.

"I've done some research of my own," Broularid said, "and I'd suggest the only reason we've not crossed with Raven before is we've done so well at staying undetected."

"Once he learns—"

"No, Monique, he cannot learn anything. We must eliminate him while he remains confused. How soon do you expect Mr. Cord to deliver?"

"I check with him in 24 hours for an update."

"Good. Tell me everything after you do. We will require men with special talents. Hopefully better than the ones we employed in California." Broularid drained his glass. "Another?"

"No." She hadn't finished her first yet.

The Frenchman stood and went for a refill. He took his head again and leaned forward with his elbows on his knees. He asked Monique to look at the tablet again.

"Scroll two times right."

She passed her finger over twice. When the last snapshot of the Venom missile plans passed, the picture of a man appeared. Dark hair, thick mustache, chiseled features. He looked around 60 years of age.

"Who is this?" Monique said.

"Your next target."

She frowned at him.

"I won't have you idle," Broularid told her. "The man you see is Noel Lalande, head of a defense firm here in France with offices in Paris. You get to work closer to home this time."

"And?"

"They are developing a new set of engines for the next generation fighter jets our air force will soon deploy. We require the specifications. Same as always. We also need samples of the prototype fuel system, as these engines will be highly efficient and, supposedly, burn less fuel."

"*Not* the same as always."

"You will get it done. If Lalande won't cooperate, he has family we can use for leverage. But, as always, befriend him first, tell him of the vision; he may join same as Denosha and most of the others."

Monique finished her drink and set the glass on the coffee table between them. "Send me his dossier," she said, "and his family's, too. I'll get to work."

"Of course."

She stood, and looked down at him. "Will there be anything else?"

"We're done. Do drive carefully back to the city. And good luck. On *both* your tasks."

She mumbled good-bye and left the library. A member of the chateau staff intercepted her in the hallway to escort her to the front door. Monique never felt so relieved to be back in her car when she climbed behind the wheel moments later. She steered for the gate at the end of the long access road; when she passed through, she made a right turn and put on speed.

22

I AM NOT YOUR FATHER.

Monique flinched at the statement for good reason.

Her father, Marco Choffron, had been a high-ranking member of *Le Milieu*, the French mafia. His crew worked as a go-between for drug runners wanting to get product from France to Greece and points south. A tough, cold man, physically and verbally abusive to both his wife and daughter, he'd never attempted to keep his only child out of the syndicate. Instead, he encouraged her, eventually placing Monique in charge of dealing with his Greek contacts.

When a shipment of cocaine on its way to Greece vanished, intercepted by rivals, Marco blamed his daughter. He accused her of bad planning and failure to vet her crew; one of them had obviously betrayed them. Monique argued they were trustworthy, and put the blame on her father's inability to secure his communications. He hadn't appreciated the back-talk. He turned her over to two thugs and ordered them to "rape some sense" into her, and it was then that Monique snapped after the years of abuse. Using a compact Walther PPK .380 concealed in a belly band under her shirt, she shot the two thugs dead and used the remaining four bullets on her father. Exit Marco.

Monique worked on her own for a while, escaped a human trafficking charge on a technicality, and then not only her father's crew but the whole of *Le Milieu* put a price on her head for killing her father. But she wasn't on the run for long. The Frenchman entered her life. He recruited her into the Source and provided sanctuary. And whatever he told the syndicate removed the kill squads from her backside and the bounty as well. Nobody kills the boss and gets away with it, unless someone *more* powerful than the boss intervenes.

She still didn't know the true extent of Broularid's strength, but she was learning more as time went on.

After leaving the chateau, she drove back to the city, and eventually parked down the street from Ramon's apartment on Rue Anatole de la Forge. In the elevator, she waited till she was halfway to the fifth floor before hitting the stop button. She tugged her blouse out of her skirt, reached up the back to unhook her bra, and slid it out through her right sleeve. She jammed the bra in her purse and hit the GO button. The elevator stopped on the fifth floor and she went down the hall to Ramon's door. She rang the bell and began unbuttoning her blouse. When he answered, a glance at the goods muted his startled reaction at her unexpected arrival. She shoved through, kicked the door closed, and told him to get out of his clothes.

Ramon didn't argue.

"THIS WAS NICE," Ramon said later, "but you need to get off."

She laughed. "I already did."

"I mean get off of *me*. I'm going to be late for work."

She only complied after he pinched her bottom. With a yelp she rolled off of him, but remained in the tangle of sheets. She watched him get up and gather his clothes from the bedroom floor. He took a five-minute shower while she lay on her back feeling relaxed for the first time in months. Broularid believed in her. She'd make him proud the way she'd never managed with her father.

Ramon emerged from the bathroom fully dressed with his hair still damp. As he combed his hair in front of the mirror, he said, "Will you be here when I get back?"

"Is there anything to eat in this apartment?"

"Of course. Whatever you find is yours."

"I'll be here. My next assignment is here in Paris so I may be in your bed more often than not."

Ramon set the comb on the cluttered dresser and smiled at her in the mirror. "Should be nice."

"It will be," she said.

He leaned over her for a kiss good-bye, and left to run the nightclub. Monique enjoyed being alone in the big bed and then wondered about the food situation. She threw on a bathrobe and went to the kitchen to investigate.

RAVEN ARRIVED at his hotel in Paris and let his eyes wander the lobby during the check-in process. He noted several cameras watching the lobby activity, and a crew worked on hands and knees to lay new tile in a roped off section. Signs in French and English said "Pardon Our Dust—We're Creating a Better Experience for You." He wondered if Monique and her gang were sophisticated enough to tap into the security feeds of various hotels to see if he had arrived; more than likely, they had connections who would pass the word. Or did it matter since Wilson was feeding information to Callen Cord who in turn was passing it along to the enemy? He didn't want to waste time looking for them. If they came to him, so much the better.

In his room, he left the drapes across the window closed and carefully unpacked, then set about unlocking the X-ray proof bottom of his main suitcase. He pulled out the Nighthawk Custom .45 autoloader, his shoulder harness, the spare and magazines. From the first of two boxes of ammo, he loaded the magazines and the gun. His trigger finger had an itch he wanted to scratch at the first opportunity. Wouldn't be long now.

His most recent trip to Paris, a few months back, had not gone well. Raven and a pal found themselves in the middle of a terrorist attack near the site of the Bastille, and while they dispatched the shooters and kept them from killing as many as they'd planned, the effort put a target on his back. Luckily, those who wanted him dead were not in no position to ever revisit the situation.

But Paris was no longer the Paris of old, of legend. The growing population turned it into just another city, crowded, dirty, with no resolution forthcoming for the homeless or traffic problems or the lack of space for incoming immigrants. The sights and tourist spots remained, but their magic had faded. To Raven, it was simply another city like so many others. They all blurred together eventually.

He frowned at the drapes. The view was probably nice, but the enemy was out there. He wasn't going to make it easy for them to get a sniper shot through the glass. He left the drapes closed, grabbed his key card, and went down to the lobby to try the hotel restaurant.

The hotel restaurant served a very good filet mignon and Raven sat at a back corner table to watch the entrance and part of the lobby.

He had a local contact named Ike Galeri, a shady street

character with fingers in many criminal pies, but he was reliable and not a rat. Raven only had to make sure nobody followed him to the as-yet-unscheduled meet. Since Galeri kept late hours, he didn't think the fellow was awake yet. He'd wait a few more hours before calling.

He ate quietly and wanted to enjoy the peace a little longer. Before the war continued in earnest.

23

RAVEN TIGHTENED HIS SHOULDER HARNESS AND PRACTICED two draws from under his jacket. He stowed the gun, checked his wallet for the room key card, and departed.

Cutting through the lobby shops to a side entrance, he stepped out and looked both ways. Traffic heavy, pedestrians paired or in groups; somebody behind him said, "Excuse me," and Raven cleared the doorway. The lone man who passed turned left. Short, loose jeans, old jacket and worn tennis shoes. Raven frowned at the man's back and cursed his mistake. He'd left himself exposed in the doorway. If the man had been an assassin, Raven would be bleeding on the side-walk by now.

Raven turned right, staying close to the building. He had an hour before meeting Galeri. Plenty of time to see if anybody had picked up his trail. He wondered if he'd see the short man in the loose jeans again.

He walked around the block three times, noting faces, postures, clothing details, to see if anything repeated. When he spotted the short man in the old jacket a second time, he grinned. Monique and her crew worked fast. As he'd expected. He went up another block and circled it twice. This time, the short man didn't show, but another lone man stood out from the rest. With most people on the sidewalk side-by-side or in groups, singles immediately looked suspicious.

The second watcher had curly hair and glasses; he wore the curls long and they stopped at his shoulders. Raven caught him a third time on his next circle of the block. Where was the short one?

The next block. Short man again. Three rotations this time, and Raven saw the curly-haired one again. This time, he had a friend, a baldie, taller than both Short and Curly. Raven frowned and crossed a street with no particular destination in mind. Why so easy to spot the watchers? Were they decoys for him to catch while a real team did the hard work? Maybe the enemy was sharper than he gave them credit for at first glance.

The street remained busy and Raven used the other people around him for cover. He turned left and hurried down an alley to the other side of the street, walked two more blocks, and hailed a cab. Raven gave the driver an address ten miles away, a spot he'd picked at random on a map. He was going nowhere near his meeting till his backside was clear. The cab driver did his best, but traffic remained slow. The delay made it tough to spot cars trying to keep up.

Presently, speed increased and Raven glanced back now and then but nobody seemed glued to the cab's bumper. He shook his head in frustration. They'd know better than to behave like amateurs. He'd need to work a little harder to clear his trail.

At a stop light, Raven tossed a few bills to the driver and hopped out despite the driver's protests. Raven dodged bumpers on his way to the sidewalk. He entered a small café, ignored the waiter who tried to get his attention, and cut through the kitchen to the rear exit. He stepped into the back alley and hurried to the right, reaching the sidewalk and joining the flow again. After two blocks and no sign of watchers, short, bald, curly-haired or otherwise, he found another cab and gave the driver the same address he'd given the first.

He powered down the window a little to let a blast of fresh air inside. He was sweating under his jacket, the shoulder harness felt tight across his back and shoulders, and he was itching for a fight. But Rule Two—no gunfights in public—held him in check. The time would come; not now. He shifted his shoulders for relief, but it did no good. Hazards of the lifestyle.

The cab let him off where Raven indicated and Raven found a bench to sit on and catch his breath. There were fewer people around; during the day, the area was a tourist spot. He noted the cars, kept an eye on passersby, yet saw no sign of anybody observing him or trying to appear like they had no interest at all.

He sat on the bench for a half hour. He was going to be very late to his meeting, but Ike wouldn't abandon him right away. Raven finally left the bench and walked two miles where the crowd and nighttime busyness returned. He found another cab and gave the driver an address near the Seine.

Raven smelled Ike Galeri's foul Turkish cigarette before he found the man. Galeri waited near a pedestrian bridge over the Seine, sitting on the shore close to the water. Raven left the sidewalk and called Ike's name. The traffic noise from the passing expressway almost drowned out his greeting.

Galeri turned, flashed a smile, and ground out his cigarette. He stood and he and Raven shook hands.

"You made it." Galeri sported a bristly beard and denim clothes.

"Had to shake some bad company," Raven said.

"You're clear?"

"Yes."

"You're sure?"

"I wouldn't have come if I wasn't."

"Based on what you asked me to look up, it sounds like you'll be diving back into infested waters."

"I want the fight on *my* terms, Ike. What did you find out?"

Raven had asked Galeri to gather any information he had on Ramon Crozier, Monique's boyfriend, and owner of the Cozy Club. Galeri took out his cell phone and showed Raven some pictures.

"Here is the club, closed during the day. Crozier has a side job selling information to high bidders, usually to spies not friendly to the West." Galeri scrolled to another. "His apartment. Fifth floor, number 506."

"Does he work for himself?"

Galeri nodded. "I've crossed with him before. Former French army intelligence. He kept up with his old contacts."

"Okay. What else?"

Galeri scrolled again. "Some social media stuff. Him and the woman. This *is* the one you call Monique, correct?"

Raven nodded. "It's her."

"She has an interesting history."

"I'm aware."

"The rumors about her father are true. She *did* kill him, and the syndicate slapped a bounty on her head. They wanted to wipe her out. But somebody intervened to make it all go away."

"Who?" Raven said.

"No idea. Nobody knows. But somebody with more power than the syndicate."

"Which means this caper isn't Monique and Ramon

working on their own. They answer to another who's calling the shots."

Galeri shrugged.

"Ever been to the Cozy Club?" Raven asked.

"It's very popular," Galeri said. "Lots of pretty girls."

"Can you get in dressed as you are?"

"What's the matter?"

"You look like a lumber jack at the end of a long month," Raven said.

Galeri scoffed and waved off Raven's remark. "I know the head chef."

"I'll buy the first round," Raven said.

Galeri laughed. "Daddy told me never to turn down free booze. Come on, the car's up the road."

Raven followed him.

24

THEY FOUND A SMALL TABLE IN A CORNER NEAR THE BAR. IT was an unwanted table, too far from the dance floor, covered by too many other bodies, for anyone to see and be seen if they occupied the space. Raven didn't mind; he had a clear view of the bar and, better, the second-level office. Lights burned inside the office, and now and then a head appeared in the window to look down. *Hello, Ramon,* Raven thought.

A DJ on the stage played loud thump-bump EDM which the crowd on the dance floor gyrated to. Full tables, a lot of liquor; men in casual clothes while the women went for skin-tight and low-cut. Lights above bathed the club in a mix of red softened with white. It seemed like an odd combo to Raven, but there must have been a method to the madness. Maybe the red made everybody hungry. The wait staff delivered as much hot food as they did booze.

"What do you think?" Ike Galeri asked, raising his voice over the loud music.

"I think Crozier's office must be soundproofed."

"Told you about the women."

"You weren't wrong," Raven agreed.

"Wish I was 20 years younger!" Galeri laughed.

"Cut off the beard and throw on a suit and I bet you'd do okay," Raven said.

"You think?"

Raven shrugged. "Can't hurt to try."

"I'll think about it."

Raven counted at least three floor managers, big men in suits who roamed and watched to keep order and make sure nobody was touching somebody they shouldn't or causing other problems." Now and then one of the floor managers visited the bar, talked with one of the bartenders a moment, and moved on.

He didn't note any other security, but figured they were stationed somewhere. If he went up the steps to Ramon Crozier, they'd show themselves. *No gunfights in public.* There'd be no need for fireworks. Any security the club employed would overwhelm him, and while Ike was no slouch in a fight, Raven had no desire to get him into trouble and on the police radar.

Raven said, "See any cameras?"

Ike pointed to the ceiling. "They're around, concealed so nobody sees them. Didn't you smile for them when we came in?"

"If they identified me, our watcher friends are on the way."

Ike scoffed. "I ain't been in a fight in a long time. I'm kinda going through withdrawal."

"Be careful what you wish for." Raven drank some of his martini. He'd specified gin, and it was cold and strong.

Raven watched the second-level office, watched Ramon work when he appeared in the window, and noted he was alone. No sign of Monique Choffron.

"Let's finish," Raven said, "and get out of here. If I'm going to talk to Ramon, I'll do it at his apartment. No good here."

Ike nodded. He downed his brandy.

"WE'VE PICKED UP A TAIL, RAVEN."

Raven reached for his gun and checked the chamber, put up the safety and slipped the weapon back into the shoulder rig. "How aggressive?"

"They're weaving around to keep up," Galeri said with a quick glance in the rearview mirror.

"Get us somewhere we can handle this," Raven said. The late hour meant much less traffic; a development both good and bad. The enemy felt emboldened to attack. Raven wanted to oblige and send back a message of his own.

But the rules applied.

Galeri said he had a place in mind and accelerated.

RAVEN TURNED in his seat to look out the back window.

"Persistent, aren't they?"

"Hang on," Galeri said.

The bearded man made a sharp right, leaving the lighted roadway behind for the darkness of a wooded area amidst the urban Paris spread.

Raven sat forward and nodded in approval. *Parc des Buttes Chaumont.* Sixty-one acres of trees and grass and nobody around at such a late hour.

Raven looked back again. The headlamps of the pursuit car bounced as the vehicle left the roadway to follow them.

"You armed, Ike?"

"I got something," Galeri said.

"Good." Raven spotted a cutout within some trees on the right. "Pull in there. Let's show 'em what we got."

Raven took out the .45 as Galeri aimed for the cutout.

TWO SHOTS POPPED from the chase car.

Raven rolled out of Galeri's car as the shots smacked into the rear glass, one pop, a second; spiderweb cracks appeared where the bullets struck. Raven hated fighting in the dark, and the park was indeed *in the dark*. No city lights penetrated the tree cover. What little light existed burned in small trail-side lamps. The glow did not spread very far.

Raven lined up on the glowing night sights of his .45 and returned fire, two rapid blasts designed to drive the enemy to cover. Raven caught Galeri's hurried exit from the car, and he carried something in both hands. A long-arm, not a handgun. Raven wanted to know what kind of hardware his buddy had brought to the fight, and had the answer two seconds later.

The whispered crackle of a submachine gun action joined the night sounds, and a string of impacts smacked into the enemy car, tearing into plastic and metal and stabbing through glass. An SMG with an attached suppressor. *Very good, Ike*, Raven thought.

He shifted on the soft ground below him. Galeri's car still covered him as he lay prone. Raven rose, sticking his head up briefly, to get the lay of the fight. The dark bulk of the car. Moving shadows blending together. He ran to the Galeri's car. Another salvo of enemy gunfire whistled overhead. No muzzle flash or sign of a gunman. He held his fire.

He wasn't the only one to hold back.

Hurried, stomping footsteps—the enemy moving.

"Ike!"

"Yeah, boss."

"Coming to ya!"

Raven scooted back from Galeri's car and fired once, then twice, where he sensed movement. The enemy fired back as he ran across an open space to the trees where Ike Galeri waited with his HK MP5K. Ike fired a burst to cover Raven's sprint. Raven rolled to a stop behind Galeri and crawled beside him.

"Where'd you get the SMG?" Raven asked.

"Back seat. Hidden compartment."

"Nice."

"This is no place for a fight."

Raven agreed. Dark and isolated was one thing, but the park was the extreme. They'd be sniping at each other all night without a victory at the rate they were going. Plus, an extended fight would bring the police.

"Keep 'em busy," Raven said.

"I got plenty of ammo for that," Galeri said.

Raven turned and crawled away from Galeri, staying close to the edge of the tree cluster, working his way around to the other side where he might get the drop on the enemy trio. He guessed it was Baldy, Shorty, and Curly, anyway; the original crew might have been replaced. But he had only seen three figures exit the enemy car. At least they hadn't brought more shooters.

Raven moved carefully through the overgrown grass. It was soft and rustled quietly as he moved. There was no way to make his progress silently. Galeri fired another salvo; louder return fire replied, Raven's ears pummeled with the sharp reports. He couldn't tell where the shooters were, but the volume suggested he was close. Closer than—

The grass ahead shuffled and parted and both Raven and the other man froze as they found themselves inches from each other and attempting the same maneuver.

Raven snapped his right hand out, extending the .45, as the other man tried to get his gun into action. Raven fired first. The explosion of the hot .45 auto shook the ground. The enemy gunner's face cratered under the impact; Raven didn't stick around to view the aftermath. He scrambled around the gunner's body and rose halfway to meet the next shooters pivoting his way.

Raven fired twice, dropped and rolled right. He slapped a full ten-round mag into the Nighthawk, pocketing the half-empty original as he searched for the third and final target. Footsteps stomped the ground. On the left!

"Ike!"

Galeri let out a yell and a shot racked, but noises continued. The grunts and smacks of hand-to-hand fighting. Raven ran. He cleared the other side of the trees and found the two figures locked in close combat, Raven yelling for Ike to get clear, the bearded man ignoring the order as he instead drew a shiny knife from the sheath under his denim shirt.

Galeri and the last gunman toppled to the ground and continued their struggle, the gunner getting a few good hits, Galeri trying to break the gunner's hold on his knife arm. Galeri bashed his forehead into the other man's nose; with a scream, he let go of Galeri's knife arm and the bearded man plunged the blade into his opponent's chest.

Galeri jumped to his feet and brushed the dirt and grass off his clothes. "You hurt?" he asked Raven.

"Are you?"

"We can talk about this in the car."

Galeri grabbed his fallen SMG and they ran to the car. The soundtrack of police sirens grew in the distance. Galeri drove out of the cutout and followed the road ahead. Raven didn't ask him where they were going. He let the bearded man drive as he knew the area better than Raven.

Raven tried not to look back. He didn't want to know if the police were gaining.

25

"DID YOU RECOGNIZE ANY OF THEM?" GALERI ASKED. THEY were through the park and back on city streets with two bullet holes in the back window but no cops bothering them about it.

"I met one face-to-face," Raven said. "Fellow I nicknamed Curly. Yes, it was the three I had to shake before meeting you at the bridge."

"It's probably not a good idea to go back to your hotel."

"Got a place in mind?"

"Crash with me tonight and we can check out your hotel in the morning."

"Fine idea," Raven said.

Galeri drove on.

"THEY FAILED."

"They *what*?" Monique said into her phone. She turned from the stove where Ramon was making crepes for breakfast and hurried into the living room.

"Raven had help," Broularid said.

Monique drew her bathrobe tighter but didn't know why. *Protective instinct,* she decided. *You need body armor.*

"Who was with him?" she asked.

"We're looking at the video to identify the man," Broularid said.

"Where did the video come from?"

"Raven and the other man stopped at your boyfriend's nightclub."

Monique felt a chill.

"We're working on a new angle of attack," the Frenchman told her. "My contact in the US says an FBI agent named Kayla Blaine is friendly with Raven, and talking with the CIA man, Wilson. She may be of use to us."

"Cord hasn't reported this."

"My contact is closer. But ask Cord why, Monique. He should know."

"I will."

"I've sent operatives to San Francisco to watch the FBI lady. Once they've noted her movements, I'll order them to attack."

"Okay." She had no idea what else to say.

"Carry on, Monique." Broularid ended the call.

Monique set her cell on the coffee table and returned to the kitchen. Ramon slid the finished crepes onto plates and gestured to the fruit toppings they'd cut up earlier. He frowned. "What's wrong?"

"It shows?"

"All over your face."

They sat and Monique told him about the Frenchman's phone call.

"Do you think Cord is holding back?"

"He's spying on his own people. He needs to be careful. I'll find out when I check with him later this afternoon."

"Do you think Raven knows about my apartment?"

"He's looking for *me*, not *you*."

"He'll find *you* by watching *me*."

She frowned as she swallowed a sip of coffee. "We might use that to our advantage."

"How?"

"I'll think of something. We know he's not a shoot-on-sight type of operator, so we can play with him a little. Give Mr. Raven enough bread crumbs to put him *exactly* where we can dispose of him. No amount of help will save him when we do."

They washed the dishes and Monique took her shower. She used the time under the hot spray to think about tasks other than Sam Raven. Broularid had said, "Carry on," and she knew what he meant.

She had to make her approach to her next target, Noel Lalande. Thinking about how to get up close with the French defense contractor gave her an idea for the Raven problem, too.

She finished her shower with a smile. Solutions always presented themselves if you gave a problem enough time.

RAVEN WATCHED Ramon Crozier's apartment building from across the street. He sat beside Ike Galeri in Galeri's car.

The hours after the gunfight in the park had been long indeed. Raven and Galeri first took his car to a garage where nobody asked questions and they replaced the rear window. Raven noted other mechanics stripping cars for parts and altering VIN numbers and license plates but a raised eyebrow from Ike kept him from pointing out the obvious. Sometimes one had to swim with the bad guys to catch bigger bad guys.

When Ramon's Mini finally pulled out of the curbside parking space, with both Ramon and Monique inside, Raven told Ike to sit tight and exited the car. He hurried across the street at a brief break in traffic and slipped through the entrance. He'd have expected Ramon to have an apartment building with a doorman, unless he thought the place was low-profile enough to avoid the extra interaction with staff who might get curious about his business.

Raven's lock picks made getting inside easy, but as he stepped through the doorway, he had to search for the next obvious obstacle. An alarm box. Raven doubted there'd be one. Alarms brought attention and sometimes sent alerts to the police. Somebody on the border of the law like Ramon Crozier wouldn't want any police involvement whatsoever in his affairs. He had other ways of handling problems, Raven figured.

Raven shut the door. The walls of the entryway displayed paintings, not alarm boxes. And those needed to be close to the door so a homeowner could punch the cancel code before the noise went off.

He started in the kitchen. Very clean, dishes stacked in a wire rack beside the sink. Enough dishes for two. He wondered how long Monique was staying and where she lived. Another question for Ike later. Raven hadn't thought of asking earlier.

Raven examined the dining table. Nothing fancy. Formica top, chairs showing their age. A right turn into the living room. More cleanliness, but a rumpled blanket sat atop another folded Afghan on one end of the couch. No dust on the TV screen.

Down the hall; he stopped at the hall closet. Shelves packed with labeled boxes, various electronic items, stuff Crozier wanted packed away instead of sold. Two bedrooms and a bathroom at the end of the hall. The bath counter had more female hair products and associated items than male.

Master bedroom needed attention. Bed not made; clothes thrown on the back of a corner chair. Female clothes.

Jackpot in the guest room. A spread of glossy black-and-white photos lay on the tightly-made bed, the opposite of the master. Raven frowned as he examined each picture. The man most featured meant nothing to him. Raven snapped pictures of the pictures with his cell phone. A map of Paris on the wall with a circle caught his attention. He snapped a shot. He was grinning when he left the apartment and used the lock picks to re-lock the door. When he returned to Ike Galeri's car, and dropped into the passenger seat, he still had the grin on his face.

"What's so funny?" Ike asked.

"They've set a beautiful trap. It's so obvious I'm tempted to tell them I know exactly what they're doing."

"Now I'm curious."

Raven showed Galeri the pictures. "I think it's Monique's next target, or they want me to think so. Recognize this man?"

Galeri pressed his lips together, which only made his thick beard cover his mouth entirely. "No, never seen him. But we can find out who he is super easy."

"I can do an image search."

"You could do that, too."

"It's what you were thinking, weren't you?"

"Well—" Galeri grinned.

"All right. Let's run by my hotel and see the situation there, then we'll find out who Mr. Mystery might be."

Ike started the car. As they sat in traffic, Galeri said, "If you know it's a trap, why are you walking into it?"

Raven, using an image search, uploaded a picture of the

man in Monique's photo set. "What you really mean to ask is what if the fellow in these photographs is a diversion."

"Sure."

"He might be. Based on these search results, I doubt it."

"Who is he?"

"Noel Lalande, CEO of Arsenal Lalande. Ring a bell?"

"Nope."

"Let's see what the internet says." Raven typed the company name into the search engine. He read the first two articles on the results page. "Seems legit," he said. He scrolled through more results. He'd take time later to read through more and study the company properly.

"What if he's a diversion?" Galeri asked.

"Might be. We will see," Raven said.

"You're more interested in having fun with them than avoiding trouble, aren't you?"

"Yup," Raven said.

Ike Galeri laughed.

26

SOME DAYS IT HURT TO GET OUT OF BED.

Noel Lalande's back ached, and so did his feet. As he rose from his bed, the soreness of his heels flared; he winced. A career as a French paratrooper with hard landings associated with jumping out of perfectly good airplanes caught up with him years ago as his age advanced. The pain was getting worse. There was nothing fun about being 70-years-old. The impacts had affected his back, too. He handled the pain with dignity, but soon, for sure, he'd need a doctor to help him manage it better.

But he was proud to have served his country the way he had.

As always, the noise his wife made while cooking breakfast woke him. She banged and clanged frying pans and other cookware—but at least she made a good breakfast.

A hot shower helped ease the aches and pains. Advil helped further if it became really bad in the afternoon, but he preferred not to overload his body with pills. By the time he arrived in the kitchen, Alizee had the food on the table. He wore his usual suit and tie; it was his uniform, and as important as the military uniform he'd work for so long. He parlayed his military career into a consultation job with French defense firms, eventually becoming CEO of his own company. He planned to keep the chair until he retired in five years. He saw no reason to stop sooner.

He kissed his wife good morning and thanked her for the food. Today was a couple of eggs and toast and his usual honeydew slices along with black coffee. They didn't talk about work; much of what Lalande did at the office was classified. Alizee wasn't interested anyway. Their daughter, currently away at university, was coming to visit over the weekend, and Alizee wanted to make sure her husband didn't have a morning golf game or any business which might keep him away from the family outing she had planned.

Lalande was used to his wife taking charge of a schedule and running off like a kid who'd stolen a handful of candy, but he'd planned ahead and canceled appointments or made sure his associates knew not to expect him for tee time. As it was, he hadn't seen his daughter in at least three months. She had not had an easy start to college, and he wanted to see how she was getting on. He hadn't liked university, either. He found the structure and hierarchy of the university system a hindrance to his own ideas of what he wanted to do with his life. The irony of his military career, where he followed strict orders in a not-perfect institution of its own, always made him smile. But he'd found his calling in uniform. It was different than sitting in a classroom.

Lalande and his wife enjoyed a quiet breakfast, and then he departed for the office. He promised he'd be home at his usual, punctual, six o'clock.

GETTING the man in the pictures identified via an image search was easy, but finding where he lived required more legwork for Ike Galeri. But he located the CEO's home. Raven, alone in a rental car, waited down the street from the Lalande estate. When the CEO departed in a white four-door Mercedes, Raven started his own car and followed.

The estate was part of a quiet neighborhood north of Paris. Foret de Montmorenay overlooked part of the city. Large homes concealed behind walls; rolling green hills and patches of forest; it was the only "country living" available in the region. Traffic moved at a slow pace along a two-lane road which wound through the green hills. Raven wasn't the only person tracking Lalande. His recon of the neighborhood prior to taking his watch position showed a full surveillance team at work—the other side, proving Lalande was *not* a diversion. They had a team on the house, and a second car also followed the Mercedes. Raven let the enemy trail behind him and use his car to hide from Lalande's view. It allowed Raven to keep track of both on the two-lane road.

The drive into Paris, once they neared the city limit, went from a smooth and easy country drive to a stop-and-go rush with multiple lanes of traffic. Plenty of room for the surveillance car, a Renault, to move closer to Lalande's Mercedes. Raven was prepared to step in should they make an aggressive move, but he expected they wouldn't. The man in the passenger seat of the Renault spoke into a radio. They were only *tracking* Lalande. They weren't there to blow him off the road.

Noel Lalande was the next David Denosha.

Raven wanted to make sure he didn't suffer the same fate as his friend.

Speed picked up again when Raven and the Renault followed Lalande onto a motorway.

Raven let Lalande get ahead when they reached the city,

then fell behind the watchers in the other car. Tall buildings loomed off the motorway. Raven knew the address of Arsenal Lelande, but his goal was to learn Lalande's routine and get a sense of what the other side had in mind. He wanted to intercept and warn the CEO of the Monique Problem.

Lalande exited for more stop-and-go on city streets, and he eventually entered the basement garage of his office building. Raven followed the watchers who accelerated away from the building and turned around the block.

Were they calling it a day, or moving to another position? Maybe heading back to Lalande's home to break into the house and hold his wife hostage? *Nuts.* Raven worked his way through traffic, shifting lanes to get around other cars, and closer to the watchers. He wanted to get close to the passenger side of their car. He wanted a clear shot at a back tire.

He stayed with the Renault to the motorway they'd exited earlier. They were going back the way they'd come, which mean returning to the estate, which meant...

Raven remembered the other team who'd stayed to watch the Lalande home. The wife was the target. He felt certain.

Raven powered down the window and unzipped his jacket for easy access to his .45 autoloader. Adjusting his speed and lane position, he blocked other cars from getting into his lane. The watchers pulled ahead. *Closer.* He eyed his escape route at the same time as he measured the distance between him and them.

Closer. The rental's engine whined as the revs climbed. When it shifted, he was close enough. He drew up alongside the passenger, who still spoke into a radio. He noticed Raven and turned his head, but by then Raven was dropping back and extending the Nighthawk Custom .45 out the window. He fired once, then again. The first shot ripped through the fender, but the second scored. The tire burst, shreds of rubber flying at Raven's car as he dropped back further, then cut left and accelerated away. A glance back showed the Renault pulling to the side of the road and other drivers slowing. He kept going until he felt it was time to slow down. The French motorway cameras weren't friendly. Luckily, he'd rented the car under one of his assumed names. He'd pay the speed fines if the French cops ever managed to catch him.

He had to get to the Lalande home before the backup team executed their plan. Was the passenger on the radio communicating with them?

Hell with speed cameras.

Raven drove faster.

If he didn't make it in time, he didn't want to have to explain things to Lalande. On an impulse he took out his phone and dialed the police emergency number. He advised of a break-in at Lalande's address and claimed to be a neighbor across the street. The dispatcher promised to send units. Raven set the phone aside but did not decrease speed.

27

RAVEN RETURNED TO THE LALANDE'S NEIGHBORHOOD AND parked two blocks away from their estate. He wasn't able to get closer. French police cars, their cherry lights flashing, occupied the street in front of the gated home. Raven hoped the police presence was enough to scare away the secondary crew, unless they'd been intercepted trying to enter the house. He figured they would have waited for the Renault.

He left the rental curbside and set off across the street to climb a hill. Grass overgrowth muted his climb; trees provided cover at the top; he looked over the stone wall surrounding the Lalande property and watched.

Officers milled about the grounds making a show of searching; two spoke with Mrs. Lalande on the porch, sheltered from the bright sun under the overhang. Nothing had taken place. No violence, or a hop over the wall by the other side. But the cops had responded to his call, and Mrs. Lalande appeared none the worse for wear. The attention might have been embarrassing, but better embarrassed than dead or a hostage.

Raven stayed within the trees. He waited for the cops to

leave, which took another 45 minutes. He stayed in place another fifteen minutes before venturing down the opposite slope. The house wall stopped at the foot of the hill; it was an easy jump, albeit not a smart one. Raven jumped over the wall and landed hard on the grass on the other side. With his feet still stinging from the impact and his legs zapped from the shock, he straightened his jacket and made his way to the house. He'd have to point out the ease of entry and the security risk by having the wall so close to the hill.

At the porch, he rang the doorbell. Mrs. Lalande answered quickly, but stepped back with surprise. Raven wasn't a cop.

"Who are you?" she asked.

"My name is Sam Raven. I'm the one who called the police."

Confusion twisted her features. She looked good for her age; still thin, no sign of a facelift. She let her long blonde hair dangle down her back.

"What? I don't understand."

"I can explain. May I come in?"

"You most certainly may *not*. Tell me why the police were here."

"You and your husband are in danger. I'm trying—"

"You need to leave or the police will be here again." She started to shut the door.

"Mrs. Lalande—"

"How do you know who I am?"

"I'm an American agent," he said. "We've uncovered a plot against your husband and his company, and I called the police because I wasn't going to get here in time."

"In time for what? You're making no sense!"

"In time to stop them from kidnapping you."

She cut off her reply and frowned.

"I'm here to help," Raven said. "I can explain everything."

"Stand right there and start explaining."

Raven blinked. She wasn't afraid of him, at least. Her reaction should have been to suggest he was the one sent to grab her. She may have figured she'd have been taken already if it were truly Raven's purpose.

"There is a group of French criminals targeting the heads of defense companies," Raven said. "They're already responsible for several deaths in the US, and now they're targeting your husband."

Color drained from her face. "Why?"

"I don't know yet."

"Then how do you—"

"I followed your husband to work, and so did somebody else. I suspected the gang would strike at you to get to him, so I told the police there was a break-in here. Did they ask you about a break-in?"

"Yes. They searched the house even after I told them no."

"I'm not lying to you."

"This is a crazy story you're telling me," she said.

"It's the truth. I failed to stop them in the US and I don't want the same thing to happen here."

She studied Raven critically. He remained still and let her judge him, for good or bad. If she insisted he leave once again, he'd depart and try again. He'd talk to her husband. He knew where to find Monique, too. Stick a gun in her belly and she'd tell him everything he wanted to know.

"All right," she said. "I believe you. Come inside and tell me more."

She opened the door to allow him inside.

———

RAVEN PROVIDED MORE DETAILS, including the background of his relationship with the Denoshas. Alizee Lalande listened without comment; when he finished, she only said, "I think I need to call my husband."

She did. They spoke for two minutes. She hung up and announced her husband was on his way home. All she'd said was the police had visited and a man waited for him to explain they were in some sort of danger.

Noel Lalande rushed into the house an hour later, flushed red and worried. He embraced his wife and began asking questions; rapid-fire questions, his wife not bothering to answer but shushing him instead. Raven stood watching. Lalande didn't notice him. After the fourth shush, the older man finally snapped his attention to Raven.

"And who are *you?*"

Alizee turned him back to her and brought him up to date. Lalande went silent. Alizee suggested they sit and talk and departed to get her husband a strong drink.

Raven and Lalande sat across from each other on plush white couches which matched the white walls. It was a fancy room, hardly used, filled with the kind of hand-made furniture the rich liked to pay for. The glass coffee table between them was spotless. If it hadn't been for a blackened edge, Raven wouldn't have realized it was there.

The older man stared hard at Raven. Raven understood the man's suspicion. He was an intrusion, an unknown, and Lalande's first instinct was to fight. Raven remained silent until Alizee returned with a silver tray. A decanter of amber fluid and three empty glasses sat on the tray.

"We can *all* use a drink," she announced. She poured and handed out glasses, husband first.

"Now, sir," Lelande said, after a healthy swallow and top-off. "Explain your presence in my home."

Raven introduced himself and started once again from the beginning. He kept to the exact details he gave Alizee.

Lalande's expression didn't change much; though skepticism replaced suspicion, the hard stare didn't alter.

"I have not met this Monique person," Lalande said, "nor has anybody else approached me with this nonsense."

Raven showed Lalande his phone and a picture of Monique. Lalande shook his head.

"I have not seen her."

Raven put away his phone.

"I think you are telling stories, Mr. Raven. But I cannot fathom *why*."

"Dear—"

Lalande cut her off with a dismissive gesture. "We've entertained this foolishness long enough. You say you're an American agent? Nonsense. If you were, you would not say so."

"You have connections, Mr. Lalande. Call them. Mention my name."

"I don't—"

"Your French associates will know who I am," Raven continued. "Don't worry. When Monique does contact you, I won't be hard to find." He gave Lalande the name of his hotel and room number.

"You can bet I will conduct my due diligence on you, Mr. Raven."

"Please do. Also, please increase your personal security." Raven explained his hop over the wall. Then he stood up.

Alizee rose and escorted Raven out. Lalande remained seated. When she returned, she sat again.

"I believe him."

"I don't," he told her.

"At least do what he says."

"I will make sure you have one or two men with you at all times. I can take care of myself."

"Don't be a fool, Noel. Nicoline is coming."

"I am not a fool, and nobody is going to hurt my family." He finished his drink and set the glass on the table. He grabbed Raven's unfinished glass and downed the remaining contents as well. Letting out a breath, he told his wife he'd be in his office upstairs; he had many calls to make.

She promised to call him when she had dinner ready.

28

LALANDE CLOSED THE DOOR TO HIS SMALL DEN AND TWISTED open the blinds. Sunlight streamed into the room. Most other execs he knew enjoyed spacious home offices with plenty of furniture; almost a sanctuary away from the rest of the house. But he kept his office small because he didn't like excess. He didn't need "stuff". Alizee had insisted on the fancy furniture for the living room.

He sat at the desk facing the wall and turned on his computer. His one splurge was a large-screen monitor. He liked big fonts so he could read without his glasses.

First, he used the internet to look up David Denosha. He had never met the man, but he knew the name, and had a familiarity with Denosha products. A chill crawled up his neck when he read about the home invasion resulting in Denosha's murder only days after somebody shot and killed his wife in Washington, DC.

Next, he used the telephone, and worked the phone lines for the next two hours either talking to contacts or leaving messages.

Most of his connections in US and French intelligence

knew the name Sam Raven, and knew what he represented. They told him if Raven had seen him personally, he should pay attention to what he said.

Lastly, Lalande called the security chief at the office. He needed a few men to protect his wife.

He also needed another drink.

RAVEN RETURNED TO HIS HOTEL. Nobody trailed him this time. He ate lunch in the hotel restaurant but the sandwich sat heavily in his gut. He had nothing to show for his effort so far, apart from three dead goons which meant very little; worse, the Lalandes remained in danger. Back in his room he sat at the desk and called Clark Wilson in the US.

"I'm not surprised," Wilson said after Raven's update. "Lalande is known to be *very* stubborn."

"He might get him and his wife killed."

"Going for the direct approach now?"

"I'm uncertain," Raven said. "I don't want the big fish to get away while I'm fussing with the small fish."

"You think Monique isn't the ring leader?"

"I'm sure of it. The person in charge is whoever convinced the syndicate to let her go after killing her father. He's the person I need to find."

"You need to be careful, regardless."

"Why?" Raven asked.

"One of the three goons you shot the other night lived long enough to describe you and your buddy."

Raven cursed.

"Cops aren't working too hard to find you considering the goons were all known thugs. But they were also free-lance. Can't connect them to Monique or anybody else."

"Still. Being on the radar does not help."

"Yeah."

"What's happening on your end? Has Cord anything to add?"

"Monique is asking about Kayla Blaine."

"*What?*"

"She's been in touch with me, Sam. FBI is still working the Denosha case, and she wanted to compare notes. I think she was more interested in what *you* were doing."

"How did—"

"I did not mention her to Cord," Wilson said. "Which means—"

"The other side has a source in the building. Our play with Cord may come back to bite us."

"Don't worry about Kayla. I have a team watching her."

"How?"

"There are ways to bend the rules, Sam."

"Nothing can happen to her."

"Maybe it's time to press the small fish."

"Yeah," Raven said.

———————

THE NEXT MORNING, Noel Lalande returned to his office, putting up a strong front. He had several meetings and a conference call scheduled for the first part of the day, which meant a late lunch, and he tackled each task with focus concealing his inner anxiety. He kept thinking Raven was right during quiet moments.

But he wasn't sure he wanted to admit he was wrong.

A four p.m. sales appointment sealed his decision.

The woman who showed up for the appointment wore a sharp blazer, skirt, blouse combination and left her hair long. Lalande tried to keep his hand from shaking as they greeted each other and sat. The desk between them, Lalande realized, offered no protection from attack. He recognized the woman from the picture Raven showed him.

Monique had arrived.

———

"I'M NOT HERE to sell anything, Mr. Lalande."

"Oh?" *Keep your composure, old timer.*

"You manufacture and sell weapons of war, right?"

"No. I provide weapons for the defense of France."

"An understandable point of view, but not entirely the truth, and you know it."

"Get to the point, Monique."

"You know me?"

"I know someone who knows you and told me all about you."

"Mr. Raven doesn't know the truth. Not a shred of it."

"Explain. Convince me you're right."

"I represent an organization called The Source," Monique said. "We are a peace consortium, dedicated to stopping war. Did Mr. Raven tell you anything about that?"

"He told me you murdered several people, including two friends of his."

She scoffed. "Again, he's missing several *facts* I'm happy to explain to you."

"I'm waiting."

"You're old enough to remember a phrase from the Cold War. *Mutually assured destruction.* Or MAD. Correct?"

"I remember."

"The United States and Soviet Union maintained enough of a nuclear stockpile to make all-our war an option neither side contemplated. Why? Because there was no way to achieve victory. Any nuclear exchange meant the destruction of all life on earth. *Billions* of deaths, Mr. Lalande. Billions.

Nobody was mad enough to inflict such carnage across the globe."

"Your point remains unclear, madam."

"The Source believes if every nation has access to the same weapons and technology, war will be obsolete. Nations will be forced to talk and compromise because neither has more powerful and sophisticated weapons than the other. Fighting will be too costly. We partner with many defense firms, such as yours, such as the Denoshas, to make sure no country has the edge on another. It's still mutually assured destruction, but not necessarily with nukes. Make sense now?" She smiled.

"And you want me to join? You want me to betray the nation I have fought for in more ways than one?"

"In the name of peace, Mr. Lalande. You say you want to defend France. This way, working with *us*, you can make sure war is never again treated as another day at the office. You aren't *betraying* France; you're *protecting* France. It's noble, isn't it?"

"Explain the murders," Lalande said. "They *happened*, madam. I read about them."

"Peace comes with a price."

"You murder in the name of peace? Nonsense."

"We do what we must to maintain our mission. Notice I haven't denied anything, Mr. Lalande."

"What did the Denoshas do to deserve what *you* did to them?"

Monique shrugged. "The wife got cold feet. She was going to talk. Her husband then decided to do the same. He lost the will to do what was necessary."

"And you'll do the same to me once I've outlived my usefulness, correct?"

"No. The Denoshas are an extreme example. We prefer

things don't deteriorate to where we must make such a decision."

"What do you want from me?" Lalande asked.

"Access to the plans for the new jet engines and other current and past projects. We will offer them to other countries free of charge, and you'll have the satisfaction of knowing your daughter, Nicoline, will live in a world where everyone knows peace."

"How dare you mention my daughter." Lalande's neck flared red. "How *dare* you."

"Calm down, Mr. Lalande. The point is obvious. Fathers worry about their children. No matter how old they are. Wouldn't it be nice to know she and her future family will live in a world where war is only an unpleasant memory, a history lesson in school?"

Noel Lalande let out a sigh. She knew how to press his buttons. She'd done her research, and had probably used surveillance to find out more; in his mind, he realized a false sense of security allowed them to follow him undetected. Like they had the day before, when Raven intervened. And he wished he listened to Raven when he had the chance.

"Do you expect a decision now?" he asked.

"Not at all. You have much to think about. Take a few days."

"I can give you an answer now," he said.

Monique raised an eyebrow and waited.

"The answer is *no*. You may leave under your own power or I'll have security carry you out."

"I don't want trouble," she said. "Seriously, it's not how we have to do this."

"I know enough about how you do things, madam."

With a disappointed shrug, Monique left her chair. Lalande did not rise. She headed for the door.

"One more thing," Lalande said.

BULLET ALLEY | 155

She turned.

"I am not a man to mess with. Any violence against me and my family will be met with a swift response."

"I have no doubt," Monique said. She flashed a smile, opened the door, and went out. The door clicked shut behind her.

Lalande reached for his phone.

29

RAVEN ANSWERED HIS PHONE WHILE SITTING IN HIS RENTAL car. "Yes?"

"Mr. Raven."

"Mr. Lalande. Hello."

"She came to my office."

"I know."

"How?"

"I followed her today looking for an opportunity to grab her for questioning. I'm parked outside your building. What did she say?"

"Too much for a phone conversation. Come up to my office right now."

"On my way."

MONIQUE ALSO MADE a call on her cell as her driver steered through city traffic. She called the Frenchman with her report.

Broularid sounded disappointed.

"Too bad," he stated.

"We'll need to persuade him."

"What about Raven? He interrupted our surveillance yesterday. If he's already spoken to Lalande—"

"Let's stick to the plan. It will draw Raven to where we want him."

"I'll send a proper greeting party to collect the daughter then," Broularid said.

"Her plane lands in two hours."

Monique ended the call with a smile. *Old bastard thinks he's in charge.*

She turned to look out the window at the passing street scenery.

RAVEN INSISTED on accompanying Lalande to Orly Airport to pick up his daughter. The drive gave them more time to talk, and the pauses in between gave Raven time to think.

The story Lalande told of Monique's visit wasn't what he expected. The objectives of The Source, and their willingness to kill for peace, made no sense to him. It had to be a ruse, a cover for trafficking in hi-tech weapons. But no. They weren't *selling* the weapons. Clark Wilson had made it clear the Denosha blueprints were free. And thinking of David and Jen's involvement truly ate at him. They weren't victims; they were willing accomplices, and Jen wanted to blow the whistle because of "cold feet". He wanted to find an argument against the idea, but deep down he knew it to be true. It explained a lot of what Jen had said, the way she'd said it, and what she refused to say. Before she died.

What did he owe them now? He'd wanted the truth; he had it. He wanted revenge, but they were part of the problem. What now?

He'd come too far to pack up and go home. Plus, Kayla Blaine was once again a target. Because of him. If he didn't erase The Source from existence, they'd keep killing until somebody finally *did* stop them. *Might as well be me*, he decided.

He turned to Lalande. The older man drove, eyes focused on the road, but he looked nervous.

"You all right?"

"No."

"Slow down," Raven said.

"I didn't realize." Lalande backed off the gas.

"We're on time. Take it easy. They won't grab her in front of a bunch of airport cops at a busy terminal."

"You sure, Mr. Raven?"

"Of this, yes."

Lalande nodded but Raven knew the reassurance didn't bring an end to the old man's worry. They stopped for a red light with the sprawl of Orly Airport ahead. A jet thundered over the motorway as it aimed at the runway. Lalande urged the light to change. Raven told him to settle down. Lalande took a deep breath and tried to comply.

Finally, the light changed and he joined the flow of cars approaching the terminals. Normally Raven disliked curb-side airport pickup, but this time it had an advantage. They'd get Nicoline and her suitcases loaded into the car and be out and away quickly.

Traffic slowed. The busy activity outside the arrival terminal kept Lalande's eyes shifting back and forth. Then he spotted Nicoline near the curb.

"There she is," he announced.

Lalande double-parked. He hopped out to greet his excited daughter. She wore dark, loose-fitting clothes and a red knit cap. Her short blond hair sprouted beneath the cap. Long silver earrings dangled from each ear. Lalande grabbed her two suitcases and went to the trunk. The lip popped up. Raven felt the back of the car drop a little as the suitcases took up space; the trunk lid slammed closed and Lalande hurried his chatty daughter into the back seat. She wore a startled look; her father's urgency was out of character. An airport cop walked toward them blowing a whistle. Lalande waved as he slid back behind the wheel and drove off.

"Is something wrong, Papa?"

Lalande didn't want to answer the question. The look he gave Raven betrayed his confusion. He didn't know what to say. The truth would only alarm her.

"Just in a hurry to get you home," he told her.

"Who's your friend?"

Raven turned in the seat and introduced himself. His jacket fell open a little. Nicoline's brown eyes widened at the sight of the .45 pistol in the shoulder rig. She snapped her attention back to her father.

"Where's Mom?"

"Back at the house, hon."

"Oh. Okay."

She didn't believe him. Lalande swallowed hard. Raven gestured for him to watch the road. Steady on. It was all they could do.

"Keep an eye on our backside," Raven advised, keeping his voice low.

Forty minutes to home. If traffic remained good. Lalande followed Raven's instructions and checked the rearview. He saw cars. Plenty of cars. Raven told him to look for the same car or multiple appearances of the same cars over time. Monique's gang may not have made a move at the airport, but striking during the ride home remained a strong possibility.

Lalande said he'd feel better once they cleared the city and reached the A 86 motorway. When they did, Lalande still didn't relax. Raven didn't blame him. Traffic was at least lighter, and Lalande accelerated around several cars until there were only a few vehicles in the lanes ahead.

"Why are we going so fast?" Nicoline asked.

"Don't you want to get home?" her father said.

"In one piece, yes."

Lalande moved to the right lane for the transition to the A 15.

Raven looked back.

"I think we're okay," Lalande said.

"Papa!"

"Nica, *please*. Let us concentrate."

"Tell me what's going on! Why does this man have a gun?"

"It's okay, Nica. Just taking precautions."

"Terrorists or something?"

"Something," Lalande muttered.

His eyes darted to his daughter's reflection in the rearview. She stared at him. Explaining the problem in the car wasn't how he wanted to tell her. He wanted her home and safe where he had armed security to protect against Monique and her veiled threat.

It happened in the roundabout prior to the Avenue de Paris exit.

Lalande eased into the roundabout and started to turn left. The driver of the beat-up gray van ahead of them braked hard. The van's tires squealed. Lalande braked with a startled curse, and the front end of the Mercedes crumpled into the back of the van. Lalande smacked a hand on the steering wheel.

Nicoline screamed as a second car plowed into the back of the Mercedes. The impact jolted all three, and as Raven reached for his seatbelt buckle to exit the car, two men with automatic rifles emerged from the van. Two more with the same type of firearms jumped out of the second car.

Lalande put up his hands and yelled, "Don't shoot!" through the glass. Raven kept his hands raised as well. One of the gunners fixed the muzzle of his auto rifle on Raven's face. If he went for the .45, Raven had no doubt he'd be shredded by a burst of rounds before he cleared leather.

The two gunners in back of the Mercedes moved forward. Horns honked and drivers yelled but the gunners paid no attention. The thick-bodied gunner on Nicoline's side pulled on the door handle. Locked. He reversed his weapon and slammed the buttstock into the glass once, twice, three times.

Nicoline screamed and jumped in fright with each impact on the glass. She covered her face with both arms. One last smash and the glass shattered, spraying shards at her, Lalande screaming, "No!" from the driver's seat. The gunner reached through the window, hit the power lock switch, and hauled open the door.

Nicoline tried to scoot away from the big gunner's reach but the seatbelt held her in place. The gunner released the lap lock and grabbed at her. She yelled some more and tried to smack his hand away, but the blows had no effect. A hand clamped on her right wrist. She heard him say, "You fight and I'll kill you," and began to panic. Tears stung her eyes. She felt him pulling her from the car. Once her feet touched the pavement, the gunner puncher Nicoline in the stomach. She collapsed to her knees, her screaming replaced by retching; more hands grabbed her. They grabbed her to the van.

"Stop them!" Lalande shouted to Raven. Raven did not move. The first two gunmen still held their weapons rock-steady on either man's face.

"How?" Raven said, biting off frustration. "We'll all be killed. They aren't going to hurt her. They need her for leverage. Which means I can get her back. I *will* get her back."

"This is a nightmare," Lalande said.

"I'll get her back," Raven said again.

The two gunners from the second car shoved Nicoline into the van and climbed inside after her. The first two gunners retreated and followed their comrades. The van took off with another squeal of tire rubber.

Raven lowered his hands and went for his cell. He dialed the police.

Lalande stared with blank eyes at the departing van. He didn't lower his hands until Raven pulled on his right arm.

30

ALIZEE LALANDE PACED THE LIVING ROOM.

She stopped long enough to try reaching her husband again but he didn't pick up. She crossed to the front window and looked out at the yard. The gate barring the driveway remained closed. Four security officers from the company milled about the house, two inside and two out. They wore sidearms but had fast access to automatic rifles. She felt well-protected.

A police cruiser stopped at the main gate, which then swung open on its own. The car drove up the long driveway. Alizee's heart jumped into her throat; she ran outside to wait on the porch. Both hands covered her mouth.

The police car stopped at the foot of the steps. She gasped when she saw only her husband and Sam Raven in the back seat. Nicoline was not with them.

Alizee ran to her husband as he stepped out. They embraced and he told her to hold her questions as he unleashed a flurry of words. The police officer and Raven also exited the car; all of them went inside.

Sitting in the living room, the cop remaining on his feet,

Lalande told his wife what happened. Alizee tried to remain strong but began to sob. When Lalande finished, the officer stated federal authorities would be taking over, and he expected their arrival at the house soon. He let himself out and departed. Lalande didn't tell him thanks for the lift.

Raven watched Lalande hold his sobbing wife. Anger filled the older man's eyes. Raven remained cold and detached.

He knew what he had to do.

"Is this what you expected, Mr. Raven?" Lalande said.

The question pulled Raven from his thoughts. He said, "I hate to say yes."

"You made me a promise."

"And I'll keep it," Raven said, "or die trying."

RAVEN DIDN'T WANT to wait around for the French federal cops, but decided to stay because he didn't want to leave the Lalandes alone when they needed support. Protection wasn't a problem. The four security men with their pistols and rifles filled the role nicely, and all four remained outside the house to watch all four sides.

Lalande told Raven he was welcome as long as required, and Alizee retreated to the kitchen to get dinner together. She needed the work to distract her from Nicoline's abduction.

Raven told Lalande there might be trouble between him and the French feds, and explained the shooting of the three gunners. Lalande waved off the warning. He told Raven his word alone would keep him out of any real trouble with the national police.

It wasn't till after dinner when a black government car with two representatives of the National Police arrived. Like

US FBI agents, they wore suits and stoic expressions, and Lalande welcomed them into his home. The lead agent introduced himself as Bruno Brunelle, and he and his partner listened while Lalande retold of the day's event. He referred to Raven as his security consultant, and Raven spotted one agent hide a chuckle and Brunelle glance at him curiously.

Brunelle said a crew of ten would arrive in the morning to set up a monitor on the house phone for the inevitable ransom call and associated demands. Raven didn't bother to correct him. There would indeed be a call from Monique's gang, but there'd be no ransom or demands in the usual sense. They'd want blueprints, pieces of equipment—whatever they sought from Lalande's inventory.

Brunelle pulled Raven aside for a private chat once he was done speaking with Lalande.

"I should arrest you," the French fed said. He was shorter than Raven, with light hair, uncombed. His suit was pressed and creased in all the right places, and he wore his pistol on his right hip.

"For what?" Raven said.

"For that which we will not name because there isn't a cop in France who knows your name who is willing to even *try* and arrest you. Or wants to, I should add."

"Okay."

"If Lalande has it in his head to shield you, we will accept it. We'll also accept that your reputation is not unknown, and if you can help rid France of certain ungodly figures, we wouldn't be ungrateful."

"Like last time?"

"Nobody remembers last time, either. But while I'm willing to look the other way, I can only not look so far, understand?"

"I get it."

"Okay. Good talk."

"Wait. What do you know about Monique Choffron? She has to—"

Brunelle waved off the question. "We know her. Gangster's daughter, the contract, all that. Now, I ask you, who has the power to make the syndicate rescind a murder contract? Hmm? I'd like him for an uncle, wouldn't you?" Brunelle let out a chuckle.

"Whoever he is, he wields real power."

"We hear rumors of this man," Brunelle continued, "called the Frenchman, but we don't know if he is real. We don't know if he's even in France. He's a mystery. Perhaps—"

"I'll do my best," Raven said.

"Isn't the best all we can do?" Brunelle let out a breath. "It's all we can do."

Raven agreed, but only because he didn't want to argue. The best sometimes wasn't good enough; sometimes, one needed to give *everything* to get the job done.

Up to and including one's life.

WITH THE NATIONAL POLICE agents and security personnel taking care of the Lalandes, Raven took his leave and returned to the hotel. He promised to go back in the morning. He took a hot shower in his room, and his aching body told him there had been too much day. But he didn't want to sleep until he updated Clark back in the US.

It was mid-afternoon at Langley and Clark wasn't available because of a meeting. Raven called back an hour later. Wilson asked a few questions once Raven finished his update, then said: "I don't know what to think of this 'Source' business. Do you have an opinion?"

"I think it's the real deal," Raven said. "But I don't understand why David and Jen would willingly do this, and they aren't here to answer our questions. My chat with Brunelle confirms Monique doesn't work alone, they've heard rumors about a mastermind, and it makes sense he's the one we're looking for. He's the puppet master pulling the strings. Once we find him, we can shut this operation down and maybe get a few real answers."

"They need to be stopped before they murder more people."

"Including a 22-year-old woman I watched them kidnap, yeah."

"You okay?"

"I had to sit there and watch, Clark. Do you know how hard it is to follow these rules?"

"You have them for a reason, and you were right. Had you tried to stop them, those gunners would have hosed you. This isn't over. It's only the beginning."

"And when it's over," Raven said, "there's going to be a mastermind who will have wished he was never born."

31

PIERRE BROULARID, A.K.A. THE FRENCHMAN, DIDN'T MIND
being alone. After more years than he cared to remember, he
found comfort in solitude.

He no longer needed company. He saw plenty of other
humans in his work with The Source. They were enough.

Quiet jazz over hidden corner speakers filled his library.
He sat on his favorite chair, the leather worn from years of
use but still soft, reading a book of Keats. His mind wasn't on
the poet's words. He kept glancing at the cell phone resting
on the left arm of the chair. The rhythm of Keats' words had
no way to compete with the call he waited for.

Broularid knew the latest from Monique. He'd approved
the abduction. He knew grabbing the Lalande daughter
would only make Sam Raven more determined to thwart the
plans of The Source, so he needed a way to take Raven off
the board, or at least rattle him enough to force mistakes,
hesitation, a chance to kill him.

Approving the kidnapping of Nicoline Lalande had not
been an instantaneous decision. He understood the pain

inflicted on Noel and Alizee. He was a father, too, albeit not any longer. His daughter was dead.

Broularid blamed himself for the loss of his wife and child. He'd hated war his whole life. He first learned of the horrors of combat from his father, who'd battled the Nazis. He learned more from his father's friends. There was no glory, no heroes, only survivors left scarred from their ordeal, who had to find a way to live with the memories of dead friends, nightmares, and flashbacks. He'd decided there had to be a way to stop nations from fighting, but how?

He'd traveled a long road before forming The Source. Along the way, he did whatever he could to reduce the suffering, culminating in a fateful trip. Broularid took his family to Bosnia during the Balkan War. The goal: help refugees.

An independent relief organization was having trouble getting supplies where they needed to go, so Broularid and his family helped keep the supply line going. It meant being around armed men who shot at the bandits trying to steal food and medicine; Broularid hurt for both sides, the refugees in need, and the desperate who'd kill for meat or penicillin.

He faced a problem with no solution, but he'd signed up to help; he was going to help. He prayed for the bandits.

A noble cause. Valiant effort. But his family died because of his decision to bring them along. They died while at one of the refugee camps distributing medical supplies. Somebody planted a bomb—the guilty party was never determined—and the blast killed 42 people and left more, including Broularid, wounded. He learned of the deaths of his family while recovering in a hospital.

He healed physically. Mentally, not so much. His determination to end war grew tenfold, and the seeds of global high-tech arms proliferation to bring the world to a stalemate took hold.

And now, he was bringing his dreams to reality. He was honoring the memory and lives of his family. He hated taking Lalande's child from him, but he needed the CEO to cooperate. The ends justified the means.

Broularid turned a page and ran his eyes down the printed page. Keats didn't register, and his eyes jumped instead to the cell phone once again.

Then it rang.

With a satisfied sigh, he closed the book of poems and answered the call.

"Mr. Walsh. Thank you for calling. It's time we talked."

"My apologies for the delay."

"Are you in a safe location?" Broularid asked.

"I am," the American named Walsh said.

"We have a growing problem with Sam Raven."

"I know him."

Masen Walsh was Broularid's contact at the CIA. He was a high-ranking veteran of special operations who now worked on the 7th Floor in a management capacity. He was one of the few in the headquarters building who possessed a Q Clearance, the highest security authorization one could achieve. The president had such clearance; Walsh had access to everything currently going on with CIA operations. He'd been a member of The Source since the beginning.

Broularid continued. "The woman he knows in San Francisco. Kayla Blaine. I've sent people there to take care of her, but I'm going to need you to make sure word gets to Raven's friend, Wilson."

"No problem. You want him to know so he tells Raven?"

"Yes."

"We have a bigger issue with Wilson we need to discuss as well," Walsh said.

"Explain."

"Wilson filed a report with his boss about Raven being in Paris. The report noted Callen Cord is working as a double."

Broularid sighed. Treachery was everywhere. "All right. We take the woman in San Francisco. I need you to deal with Cord."

"Not Wilson?"

"Cord's death can be attributed to other circumstances. If we kill Wilson, it's another investigation."

"Consider it done."

"Find a way to make sure Wilson understands his future if he continues trying to help Raven. I understand he has a family?"

"Yes," Walsh said.

"Make sure he gets the point."

"He will."

"Thank you, Mr. Walsh."

"Anything for you, Mr. Broularid."

The Frenchman ended the call. He then returned to Keats with renewed enthusiasm and took in every word.

KAYLA BLAINE SAT with her chair turned to face the tinted window behind her. The sun was on the opposite side of the building, so she had a glare-free view of the San Francisco skyline.

Her current caseload was keeping her busy but none of the work occupied her mind like Raven's mission in Paris. And the fallout the Feds continued sorting out on the US side. The SF and DC offices combined notes and determined the person of interest in the case had fled the country. The DC office wanted to pass the case to FBI personnel at the US embassy in Paris, and let them track down Monique Choffron, but the CIA stepped in. *No dice, FBI.*

Kayla, the only agent on the case who understood why CIA put the kibosh on their effort, had to fake being upset same as her colleagues. At least it meant CIA was somehow supporting Raven, but her brief conversations with Clark Wilson had revealed no details and thus no reassurance Raven remained unharmed.

She wanted him to come back.

To her.

Kayla knew he'd never stay, but any time she spent with Raven was worthwhile.

She rotated her chair to face the cluttered desk before her once again. There were reports to write, expense forms to file, and other drudgery to try and get her mind off Sam Raven for a few more hours.

Kayla left the office at six. She never joined the flood of departing agents and staff at five because she liked watching the traffic jam at the elevators. There were only two, and it took almost till six for everybody to clear out. Only a handful used the stairwell. By the time she stepped into the elevator, she was the only one in the car. The elevator doors rumbled closed and the descent began with a jerk.

A quick walk across the underground garage to her car...

And into traffic for the long ride home. She didn't have far to go, but getting anywhere in the city during rush hour took forever. City roads were under constant construction for upgrades, road widening, or repairs to the underground MUNI tracks, which only added to the congestion. She even had roadwork going on outside her condo. Luckily, she always left home before all the loud machine noises began.

When she finally returned to her condo in the Outer Sunset District, she parked a block away on the street and walked the inclined sidewalk to her front door. Part of the street on the opposite side remained blocked off, with construction equipment in a small cluster protecting a big hole in the pavement. The crew had left behind a small van, the cabin dark.

She unlocked the knob and inserted the same key into the deadbolt, but the top lock was already undone. Had she forgotten to lock the deadbolt when she left? Kayla dropped her purse on the steps and yanked the SIG-Sauer P-229 from the holster on her right hip.

She pushed the door open and scooted to one side, her back to a corner, the entryway hall breaking off three ways. She could go through the kitchen, slink right to her bedroom, or left to the living room. Then there were the steps to the second floor. She waited instead, finger on the trigger, breathing slowly. The condo was quiet. Outside noises leaked through the walls; typical. Drapes in the living room remained closed and the portion of the room she saw remained shrouded in darkness.

You're nuts, she decided. She'd forgotten the deadbolt and needed to be more careful in the future. With a sigh she put her gun back in the holster and retrieved her purse from outside. Turning on the light in the kitchen, she set her purse near the well-used toaster oven and poured a glass of wine.

THE VAN ACROSS THE STREET, sitting silent in the midst of the construction gear, wasn't part of the street modification effort.

Kayla didn't know it, but the truck never showed up until the work crew left for the night, which was before she departed her office.

A man and a woman sat inside the back of the van. They watched glowing monitors showing various sections of the condo's exterior, but they'd faced difficulty placing the small cameras. There was so little space between one condo and another, they inadvertently captured part of the neighbors' properties, the specific problem they wanted to avoid. A few adjustments and all cameras focused on Kayla's home, but only the outside.

Roger Justice, sitting before two monitors, sipped from a cold coffee mug. The van lacked a microwave. Had they been on the job for Sam Raven, he'd have provided a microwave. Raven knew how to take care of his Raiders. But this time, he and Lia Kenisova were working for the CIA and doing a favor for Raven, so he didn't complain. It wasn't a permanent duty station.

Lia sat in the next chair watching her own set of monitors. She'd watched Kayla's entry routine and said, "Did you go in and forget the deadbolt?"

"No," Roger told her. "She forgot to turn it."

Neither of the pair knew Raven's current mission status or why Kayla Blaine was important to him. She looked perfectly capable of taking care of herself. But when Clark Wilson reached out and asked them to keep an eye on her, they didn't refuse. They were part of a trio Raven nicknamed his "Raiders" and they came when he called, as long as they were available. They had helped Raven out of potentially deadly situations many times over the years. The third member of the Raiders, Zaven Darbinian, aka "Darbo", had not been available because of what he said was another commitment. Roger knew the real story. Darbo had broken his left foot skydiving and expected to be laid up for a few more weeks.

When not working for Raven, Roger and Lia took on jobs for individuals, organization, or governments who required covert experts to accomplish specific tasks. It wasn't as if they sat around all day waiting for Raven to call. Each had their own separate specialties.

"Think she'll stay in again tonight?" Lia asked. "Girl needs a social life. *Badly*."

"I don't think the boss's lady friend has much of a life outside work," Roger said. "But you never know."

"She doesn't appear to be in much danger," Lia Kenisova, a Russian recovery specialist, knew how to scope out trouble. They'd seen none around Kayla Blaine during their surveillance. They took turns following her during the day, since she was working, but rejoined in the van for the evening watch. One or the other stayed overnight depending on who won the coin toss.

"Doesn't matter," Roger said. "This one is a favor to Raven."

"Good grief, marry him already."

"Shut up, Lia."

They shared a quiet laugh, keeping the noise down. They didn't want somebody out walking the dog to hear laughter from inside the supposedly empty van.

Later, lights began turning off in the condos lining the street. The upper floor lights in Kayla's place remained on till 11:30, then winked out. As per their routine, Roger and Lia planned to stay until 12:30, at which time they'd see who stayed overnight. But close to midnight, Roger sounded an alarm.

"Movement over the back wall."

Lia consulted her monitors. She spotted nothing out of the ordinary until, "Got 'em on the side wall. Two."

"Only one coming over the back."

Roger scooted away from his screens. He snapped an FN High Power 9mm from shoulder leather and checked the chamber. "I'll take care of this. Bring the car around."

Lia hurried to exit the van first. Her boots scraped on the pavement as she hurried to a car parked in a nearby alley.

Their getaway unit. She dropped behind the wheel and started the motor.

Roger Justice sprinted across the street. Kayla Blaine lived in a quiet neighborhood, and there was no vehicle traffic to consider. He heard Lia start the getaway car, and the head-lamps flashed over him as he passed through the beams. The condo loomed larger as he approached, and he darted around the left side. He wanted to go in behind the two Lia spotted making for the side entrance.

Glass shattered on the opposite side of the fence. Roger used the electric meter against the wall as a boost, grasped the top edge of the fence, and swung over. He landed upright as the two intruders slipped through the broken patio glass door. One of the two men, who clutched a submachine gun, pivoted to raise the SMG in Roger's direction. The FN High Power in Roger's fist flashed twice, Roger not bothering with the sights. He was close enough to point and shoot. The pair of 9mm slugs scored. The gunner fell back without a scream. Roger ducked through the glass. The enemy gunners needed to get upstairs to reach Kayla. Roger needed to stop them.

The gunner who entered from the rear ran to his leftover partner, framing himself in the doorway between the kitchen and living room. He leveled his gun at Roger. Roger hit the floor and rolled behind a chair, aiming around the side to fire twice. He fired at an odd angle, missing the gunner, his shots punching into the wall. Shards of sheetrock pelted the gunner's face. The gunner charged ahead. Roger half-rose, firing again and again; the gunner's head snapped back and he collided with a table before sprawling onto the carpet.

Roger broke right. The narrow stairway was a lousy place to go, but it was only one flight. Still, it was a bottleneck where he'd be easily trapped with no way to escape.

The third and final gunman faced the same problem.

"Kayla, incoming!" Roger shouted. He stopped at the base of the stairs. The last gunner was already at the top. He spun to fire down at Roger, but another pair of 9mm parabellums were already flying out of the FN's barrel. They dropped the gunner where he stood. His body tumbled down the steps. Roger moved aside to give the dead man room to crumple at his feet.

"Kayla!" Roger Justice stayed at the base; she'd be up there ready to open fire with her service pistol or whatever other nasty surprises she had for defending the house. "Raven sent me! Sam Raven sent me!"

"What?" He heard her yell over the ringing of the gunfire still in his ears. She appeared at the top of the steps with her pistol extended. Roger held up both hands, with his finger off the trigger of his own gun.

"Raven sent me," he repeated a third time. He stared down the muzzle of Kayla's pistol. She held the gun in a steady two-hand grip. "I got a car outside and more help. We need to go."

"Okay," she said. Kayla tucked her gun behind her back. She still wore her work clothes minus the holster. A grab for her purse and she hurried down the steps. She moved around the dead man's body without a second glance. Roger led her outside where Lia waited.

33

CALLEN CORD LET OUT A BURP AS HE PULLED OUT OF THE parking lot of J.R.'s Wood-Fired Steaks. He enjoyed an 8-ounce top sirloin with a baked potato but had no idea what to do with the rest of his night. The solitary life wasn't the best, sometimes. A few hours of TV before bed seemed the best, if inevitable, solution. He hadn't heard from Monique lately, so he didn't have work as a distraction, either.

Then he spotted the tail.

The SUV left the curb as Cord turned onto the street. The driver went too fast catching up. The vehicle fell back a little as Cord made a left turn. The SUV followed. Cord accelerated and stayed in his lane. There was on sense using traffic for cover. They were on him.

Cord carried no weapons on him, but a Beretta 92X waited in the glove compartment. It was his emergency piece, and he wondered how many rode in the SUV, and what armament they'd deploy. Cord stopped for a light. The SUV sat four cars back. He hurriedly looked around. He needed a place to make a stand. *If* he failed to shake them. No, he had to defeat them now. Had he been in charge of the team, they'd know how to reacquire him at home; he should have seen the surveillance, and cursed his lax awareness. He needed to make a stand. Send a message. But doing so didn't require a furious gun battle. There were other ways, if he could lure them into the right environment.

When you're outgunned, you need to fight smart.

The gun crew might have been sent by an old enemy, but Monique was more likely. It made sense if she'd tumbled to his subterfuge and explained why he hadn't heard from her. But how had she figured out the duplicity?

The light changed and traffic moved forward again. Cord changed to the left lane. Another turn. He knew the neighborhood well; a school nearby might be a good open space, with more than one exit, to handle a few pests. A glance at the rearview showed the SUV making the same turn; the headlamps grew in size as they accelerated toward him. Cord stepped on the gas some more. Homes flew by, the street well-lighted, the school ahead on the right.

A closed gate blocked one driveway leading onto the campus; the other lot opposite the buildings might be blocked, too, Cord realized. Before he abandoned his idea, he swung instead into the bus loop parallel to the street, stopping hard. He threw the gear stick into Park, shut off the car, and went EVA with the Beretta 92X in his right fist. Seventeen rounds against whatever the other side brought to the party.

Cord ran down a walkway leading between two buildings, closed doors of the main hall in front of him. Another walkway branched to the right. Low light, many dark places to hide. He stole a glance back. The SUV stopped behind his car. Four doors opened. Cord faced forward and ran into the dark, across a patch of grass, and into the bushes. The wall and windows behind covered his back. He flattened on the soft ground and waited for the other team to come on the field.

He hoped he didn't burp a second time.

HE WATCHED through a gap in the bushes. There were four, the lead man giving commands; he directed two toward the main hall, and took the remaining gunner along the walkway Cord had used. They stayed close to the building wall on their right, with the patch of grass and bushes to their left— where Cord watched. Both men moved slow; the dark places held as much danger for them as they had Cord, but Cord now used such a space to his advantage. One of the gunners flashed a light to scan a few feet ahead, quickly turning it off. Cord let them go halfway down the walkway before shifting his view to watch their backsides.

Two options, Cord decided. He could engage, or run back to his car and get away. The gunners carried suppressed machine pistols. Cord was not only outnumbered, but outgunned. To take them on, even split into two as they were, was suicide; plus, cops would be on-scene within minutes of the first shot. Cord wasn't sure he could complete his task before the first patrol units arrived. He waited a little longer as the two gunners reached the end of the walkway to decide which direction to go next. Cord waited a little more. The gunners turned left, heading into the middle of the campus. They passed from his sight. When he felt they were far enough away, Cord eased to his knees, then his feet, breaking away from the row of bushes. He ran to the bus circle. He hoped they hadn't tried to disable his car. There was only one way to find out.

He reached his car. Tires intact. He extended the 92X and shot out both front tires of the SUV. The snappy report of the 9mm autoloader filled the neighborhood, the echo carrying as Cord jumped behind the wheel of his own vehicle and turned the key. He kept the lights off as he powered out of the bus circle. Two of the gunners, the ones who'd gone toward the main hall, ran at him as he turned toward the street. He ducked low, but no gunfire popped into the car's body. But his shots had been heard, they'd be reported, and the gun crew might have some explaining to do when the cops arrived. With two blasted tires, they weren't going anywhere except on foot.

It was a temporary victory, though. They'd find him at home if they wanted him badly enough, which meant home was not off-limits. He found his way back to a busy street and drove nowhere near the direction of his home. At a red light, having caught his breath, Cord used his cell to dial Clark Wilson.

"What is it?" Wilson asked with a tired voice.

"Sorry to bother you at home, Clark," he said, and then explained the incident.

"I'm not at home," Wilson said. "Paris has gone off the rails and Raven's friend in California just survived an attempt on her life, too."

"We're blown."

"What do you want to do?"

"Inform Raven I'm on my way to Paris. I have a score to settle with these people myself."

"Will do. Good luck."

The light changed to green as Cord ended the call.

34

KAYLA BLAINE WATCHED THE MAN NAMED ROGER JUSTICE lock the hotel room door. The room was a large suite, decently furnished, with a second bedroom.

"Thanks for the rescue," she said. "Did Raven really send you?"

The Russian woman named Lia answered. "A friend of his at CIA called us."

"Wilson?"

"Yup."

"Wow." Kayla dropped onto the small couch facing the wall-mounted big screen. Lia and Roger set their weapons on the dining table. "What's the plan now?" she asked.

"Not sure," Roger said, "other than keeping you out of danger. We'll figure it out after we call Raven and Wilson."

"How do you plan to keep me out of danger?"

Lia said, "I hope you like being indoors and not going near windows. This is home for a while."

Kayla scoffed. "Remind me to tell you about the last time I got involved with Raven."

"They wanted to use you to get to him," Lia continued.

"You can bet he's caused enough trouble for them to make the effort."

"As long as it means he's still alive," Kayla said.

"Do you have any pets or anything we should go back for?" Lia said.

"Nothing. Well, except clothes and maybe my computer."

"We'll take care of that," the Russia woman said. "Make sure you call your boss."

"He'll wait till morning. Can we get some food sent up? No way I can sleep now. Might as well eat something."

Roger offered to figure out the food situation. The hotel's kitchen was likely closed, but San Francisco was a 24-hour town. There'd be an open diner somewhere nearby with takeout available.

Kayla sat and stared at the carpet without any awareness of what the other two were doing. This wasn't the only time involvement with Raven put her in danger, though the outcome was better than last time, for sure. Last time, she'd been alone, trapped in a van, and had to fight her way out with a captured pistol. This time, it was nice to have help.

What next? Yes, she had to tell her boss what happened; the cops would alert the FBI as soon as they learned an agent lived at the now shot-to-hell condo on an otherwise quiet street. But she also wanted to remain incommunicado for a bit, until she had reassurance from Raven he'd slain the dragon.

Or the other way around.

Lia was talking, her accented voice breaking through Kayla's thoughts. But she wasn't talking to her. She spoke into her cell. When she came over to the couch, she handed the Android phone to Kayla. The lady Fed took the phone and said, "Raven?" with a crack in her voice.

"Forgive me, Kayla, I had no idea they were there. But I am grateful. Are you hurt?"

"Only a little shaky. No holes I wasn't born with."

Raven chuckled. "Good. Sit tight and do what Roger and Lia tell you. I'm busy here. Can't say when we'll resolve the matter, but we're making progress."

She frowned. Raven was speaking in guarded tones; he wasn't alone. She thought it best not to keep him on the line.

"Keep the promise you made," she said, "and we'll catch up then."

"I've been making a lot of promises lately," Raven said. "I'll keep them all. Put Lia back on, please."

Kayla handed back the phone and Lia Kenisova resumed her conversation. Roger returned with news an all-night diner up the street would deliver. He asked Kayla what she wanted.

RAVEN ENDED the call and smiled to himself. Now he knew how Wilson covered Kayla without breaking any CIA rules.

"Who was on the phone?"

Raven turned to Noel Lalande. The CEO sat at his desk in the upstairs den. Raven stood while Lalande access files on his computer.

"Monique made a move on my home turf," Raven explained. "They failed." He frowned at Lalande's computer screen. "What do you have there?"

"Plans, technical drawings. I will have over everything to get my daughter back. Isn't this what they want?"

"We have no idea what they want because they haven't told us," Raven said.

No contact since the kidnapping. And it bothered Raven more than he wanted to admit. There was nothing "standard" about taking Nicoline. The usual abduction / ransom playbook did not apply, which was why Raven was content to let the French federal agents monkey around and not bother with them. Monique and her crew were stalling to make Lalande panic, maybe, but what were they doing to Nicoline in the meantime?

One thing Raven decided was not to fight Lalande too much. There were points to argue and points to ignore. If he wanted to hand over everything, Raven saw no need to tell him no until another solution presented a better option.

The trick was to create those better options.

"I have an idea," Raven said.

"What?"

"They'll call soon." Raven took out his phone again. "When they do, I know how we can expedite the matter to where you won't have to hand over *anything*." He dialed Ike Galeri. When the Galeri answered, Raven said, "Ike. I need some special equipment. I want to clone a phone."

Lalande frowned at Raven. But Raven smiled back to reassure the CEO and listened to Ike Galeri present options...

"I OWE YOU ONE, CLARK," Raven, on the phone again, told his CIA friend. He stood on the porch outside the Lalande home. The fresh air and greenery revived him after the stuffiness indoors.

"You owe me nothing," the CIA man said. "And I have another surprise for you. They tried to kill Cord, too. Same time they hit Kayla."

"Did he make it?"

"He's in one piece."

"What happened?"

"Monique somehow found out what we were doing. He's on his way to join you. He'd like a crack at Monique, too."

"He can wait in line. But I'll take the help."

"Tell me the latest with Lalande."

Raven did so, adding details of his conversation with Galeri.

"Ballsy, but doable," Wilson said, "if Lalande can keep his wits."

"He assures me he will. Now go home, Clark. There's no reason to wait by the phone any longer."

"I will take your advice. Talk soon."

Raven pressed the red button with a sigh. He pocketed his phone and decided to stay on the porch and enjoy the chirping birds a little longer. The Feds were on their way; soon, federal agents would crowd the house and make moments of quiet hard to come by.

35

THE WAREHOUSE DIDN'T HAVE A WORKING HEATER. IT WASN'T awful during the day, but as the sun set and the temperature dropped, they turned on space heaters to make sure the hostage wasn't any more uncomfortable than she had to be.

Monique paced while Ramon leaned against the wall. They were in a small room off the main floor. She disapproved of the location. It was owned by a friend of Ramon's, but had sat unused for months. Filth was everywhere. Monique didn't mind honest dust, but going unused for so long had not only brought dust, but trash and debris from squatters and meth-heads who discovered its empty state. Never mind the animal feces, rats, and other unpleasantness. Prior to bringing the Lalande girl to the location, Ramon's buddy made sure to get rid of any squatters, and post security to keep others away. But she wanted a new place to hide Nicoline Lalande, and fast. She said so to Ramon.

"My friend Lucien," he replied, "will think you don't appreciate him. You wanted a place Raven might have difficulty location till you were ready for him. Lucien provided it."

"He could have at least tried to get the foul odors out of here."

"The bathrooms work. We don't be here long, and you're wasting time complaining to me."

She folded her arms and glared at him. "I don't like this place, and I don't like the so-called *security*, either."

"They're reliable men. And you've set boundaries."

Monique shook her head. When she showed up with Nicoline Lalande, all eyes had shifted to the comely short-haired blonde, and all of the eyes were searching for and waiting for an opportunity to take advantage of her. Monique ordered all of them to stay away, and remained at the warehouse to see they complied. Not only did she have to suffer in an abandoned and dirty warehouse, she had to police a bunch of thugs. A damaged Nicoline Lalande was *not* in her best interest.

"You want her out of here," Ramon continued, "get Lalande on the phone and make him give you what you want."

Monique grabbed her cell from the back pocket of her jeans. She turned her back to Ramon and dialed Lalande's number.

Four rings and a pause; the rings continued. The French feds were at the house, and she knew they'd try and trace the line. Software on her phone worked with other electronic toys in Ramon's apartment to reroute the call through several locations, throwing off any trace attempts.

When Lalande finally answered, she heard his voice crack.

"Yes? Hello?"

"Mr. Lalande, it's Monique."

"You again." His voice took an edge now. "What do you want? I am willing to negotiate anything."

"I am pleased to hear you say so. We don't want much. At

first. The return of your daughter won't hurt very much. But if you fight me—"

"I'm not going to fight. Tell me what you want to do."

"Tomorrow morning. We will meet for a quiet cup of coffee at Ten Belles. Ten a.m. You will bring me the plans for your upgraded jet engine and we will discuss Nicoline."

"I will be there," Lalande said. "I will be on time."

"I'm sure you'll be able to find me. I'll wear a big hat. Black." She smiled. "Easy to spot."

"Okay." The edge vanished; he sounded resigned to an unwanted fate. Her smile faded. All Monique cared about now was results.

She pressed the red button on the phone screen and the call terminated. She wondered how the federal cops were dealing with the rerouting. She'd been on long enough for a trace had she not had the software; they were probably very frustrated.

"All set?" Ramon asked.

She turned to face him. "Yes. All I have to do is tolerate one more night in this dump. When I'm gone, I expect you—"

"I'll keep order."

"Good. And, hey, it's not all bad. At least I'm here." He grinned.

Monique scoffed and left the office. He laughed as she passed him.

———

"Do you know this man well?"

Raven shook his head. "I know *of* him, and we may have crossed paths a few years ago, but, no, I do not know him."

Raven stood beside Lalande outside the house, near the porch, waiting for Callen Cord's rental to appear at the access gate. Cord had contacted Raven upon his arrival at Orly, and Raven gave him directions to the Lalande estate.

"He's going to help?" Lalande said. He looked tired. The skin on his face appeared to sag; his posture no longer proud and erect. The phone call with Monique had drained him. Trying to keep his wife's spirits up while his were falling only added to the strain.

"He's an extra edge," Raven said. "Somebody the enemy doesn't know about."

"*They* will know." Lalande gestured at the house.

Brunelle and his agents occupied the garage. Alizee Lalande did not want them tearing up her carpet or breaking anything. Raven kept his distance, and had not expect their attempt to trace Monique's call to pay dividends. It hadn't. Brunelle hadn't seemed surprised, either. Lalande had not elaborated when the fed asked for more information about what Monique wanted in exchange for Nicoline.

"*They*," Raven said, "aren't going to have much to say about it."

"My wife—"

"Is under the false impression this is almost over. Monique won't let your daughter go with simply what she asked for. She'll want more and she'll keep Nicoline until she gets everything. You aren't coming back with her tomorrow, barring a miracle."

"I realize this," Lalande said. "I hope your proposed solution works. I do not understand this, what you called it, phone cloning?"

"By tomorrow morning, you'll know as much as me. Here he comes."

The rented Peugeot stopped at the gate, where of one Lalande's security team met the car and called the boss to make sure they expected the arrival. Lalande said into his phone, "Send him up," and the security man activated the gate and gestured for the driver to proceed to the house.

Cord stopped the car at the porch and Raven went down the steps to meet the man. Cord climbed out of the four-door and Raven extended his right hand.

"I'm Sam Raven. Welcome to Paris."

"Callen Cord." They shook hands without trying to crush each other's grips. "Nice to finally meet you."

"Likewise. Let me introduce you around the house. We'll stay out of the garage for now. This is Noel Lalande—"

Inside, after meeting Lalande's wife, Raven took Cord into another room and away from the prying eyes of the French feds. Raven went over the plan for the meeting between Lalande and Monique. Cord thought the idea of copying Monique's phone included certain risks.

"She might not carry one," he said. "Let's grab her and hook her nipples to a car battery instead."

Raven didn't laugh. "We have to do this right. A hostage's life is at stake."

"Are you sure the old man won't blow it? He doesn't look too good."

"He'll remember who he is and rise to the challenge," Raven said. "If not, we'll find a car battery."

"I knew we'd get along."

This crime, Raven cracked a grin.

"Mr. Raven!"

Raven turned away from Cord. Lalande was waving for him to come over. The French fed, Brunelle, stood next to Lalande, and looked mad.

36

"YOU CANNOT GIVE THAT WOMAN TECHNICAL PLANS TO military equipment," Brunelle said. "I will arrest you for treason."

Color drained from Lalande's face. He started to stammer, turning pleading eyes to Raven, who put a hand on his shoulder and said, "Hang in there for two minutes."

"But—"

Raven held up two fingers to silence Lalande and turned to Brunelle.

"You're right. But what if—"

"What if *what*, Mr. Raven?" the French fed said. "I should arrest you for interfering in a government investigation."

Raven ignored him. The fed was as frustrated as any of them; the usual abduction playbook wasn't working in this case, and Brunelle didn't know what to do.

"Let's change the plans. Mr. Lalande, everything is digital, right? You're not handing them paper copies."

"True," the CEO said.

"Can we alter the plans so she's not getting the real thing?"

"It will take hours!" Lalande said. "We'll be up all night."

"Then get the coffee going," Raven said. "We got drawings to change."

Brunelle said the changes *might* be acceptable. But he didn't argue very hard.

NOEL LALANDE eventually took a sleeping pill to knock himself out after several hours' worth of work on changing the plans for his jet engine design. By removing key components and substituting others, the plans no longer made any sense. He only hoped Monique didn't know how to read them.

He arrived at the Ten Belles café, briefcase containing a tablet computer with the doctored plans in hand. He arrived an hour early. He did so at Raven's suggestion, and he recognized the strategy. Arrive last to a meeting with the enemy, and you might not live long enough to leave.

He found his strength again as he waited and sipped hot black coffee which chased away his mental cobwebs. Raven's friend Ike Galeri came to the house early in the morning with a new cell phone for Lalande to keep in a pocket. All he had to do was leave the "Galeri phone" alone. The bearded man promised the installed software would do all the work once it sensed Monique's phone.

"What if she doesn't have her phone?" Lalande asked.

Galeri only shrugged. "Then it won't work."

Raven jumped in: "We have a back-up plan."

Cord stifled a laugh. He volunteered the battery in his rental car; Lalande didn't understand the joke, and Raven didn't explain.

Lalande shrugged off thoughts of the last few hours as he sat and waited. It was a warm morning. Traffic was heavy and the café busy. Lalande sat outside with his back to the outer wall. Raven wanted Monique's back exposed; it was a strategy to keep her from noticing him, Cord, and Galeri in a car parked across the street.

He thought again of the phone provided by Galeri. It looked like a normal phone, but what wasn't obvious about the device lay beneath the exterior façade.

A Bluetooth-based hacking tool ran in the background of the other functions. Galeri explained such software was available to the public should they decide to make the effort, but he had developed a proprietary program instead. All Lalande had to do was *not* touch the phone.

He sat and waited and sipped his coffee. He didn't drink too fast or too much because he didn't want to require a bathroom break before Monique arrived.

Then again, he was 70 years old.

He'd have to hold it.

RAVEN SAT in the passenger seat of Cord's Peugeot; Cord behind the wheel, Ike Galeri in the back seat with a laptop computer.

"Are you getting a signal from the bait phone?" Raven asked.

"Very strong," Galeri said. "But there are a lot of other cell phones around him. It might be tough to figure out which one belongs to Monique. I'm sure it will be the one with a signal as strong as his considering their close proximity."

Galeri's explanation of the hacking software had been more for Lalande's benefit than Raven's, but he thought about the bearded man's lecture anyway. The hacking program exploited a weakness inherent in all cell phones - the Bluetooth connection. The program slipped through the security software to make a copy of the operating system. When it was done, they'd have access to her contacts, calendar information; anything to help track down not only where Monique was hiding Nicoline, but Monique's boss as well. Raven wanted the top dog who pulled her strings. Only then could he hope to get the answers to his questions.

Galeri's laptop wasn't involved in the phone copying process, but he'd monitor the progress on his screen. They needed *everything*. Every contact and their numbers. If she had an Angry Birds score, Raven wanted it, too.

Cord said, "There she is."

Raven looked across the street. Cord had cleaned the front wind screen; nothing obscured his view. He spotted the dark-haired woman and her black hat right away.

She wasn't a woman he'd ever forget.

For all the wrong reasons.

LALANDE LOOKED up as she approached. He'd been scrolling through his phone, trying to appear natural, when her tapping heels pulled his attention from the cell screen. He tucked the phone inside his blazer pocket.

Monique pulled out the opposite chair, sat, and placed her purse in front of her. She left her black hat on her head. Lalande frowned. What did she have inside? Camera? Gun? He feared a camera more than a gun because of the potential blackmail, but then wondered how the lens could record through the leather material. *Paranoia is not going to help*, he concluded.

"You made it early," she said.

The waiter arrived; she ordered the same as Lalande. He faced her stoically, staring hard. He wanted her to make the first move. He wanted to convince himself he had the upper hand because of Raven and his associates.

"I trust there were no problems," she said.

Lalande shook his head.

Monique opened her purse and took out her phone. A couple of taps on the screen and she handed the device to Lalande.

I hope Raven's trick is working, Lalande thought. He took the phone and turned white. He wasn't thinking any longer of Raven's trick of what Galeri's phone was doing while they sat. The phone Monique handed him showed a video feed of his daughter, Nicoline, and all he wanted was to do what Monique said so he could get her back.

Nicoline sat on a metal folding chair in an empty room. Most of the room was dark and he had no idea where it might be. He was focused enough to look for stray details giving away her location, but found none. Her arms were tied behind her back, and her ankles bound to the chair legs. A bandana covered her mouth. She looked scared, uncomfortable, and Lalande had to swallow growing rage. *Do you part. Then this ends.*

"Proof of life," Monique said.

Bitch.

Whore.

Animal!

I want to kill you with my bare hands!

Lalande verbalized none of his thoughts, but he felt his stoic expression break into one of suppressed anger.

"I see her." He handed back the phone.

"She has not been mistreated. I will not let a woman be assaulted when I'm in charge. On that, you have my word."

"But?"

"Oh, but I *will* kill her if you fail to deliver. Let me see what you brought."

Lalande set the briefcase on his lap. The waiter returned with Monique's coffee as a breeze rustled the strands of hair hanging below her hat. Lalande popped open his case. He removed a large-screen tablet and opened the file on the jet engine designs he and Raven doctored. He held out the tablet to her. She made him wait while she sipped the coffee and dabbed her mouth with a napkin. A red lipstick stain smeared part of the cup's brim.

Monique took the offered tablet and Lalande placed his right arm on the table. He had forced himself to hold the tablet steady despite the tremors he felt beginning. He watched her scroll through the drawings, spread her fingers over the display to enlarge, and frown. Then the frown turned into a grin. She shook her head.

"I know you didn't have a choice, Mr. Lalande. But you should have known you can't fool me."

"The plans are accurate. They are what you asked for!" Lalande leaned forward as his voice rose; he stopped, sank back in the chair, and Monique smiled.

"How did you know?" he said.

"Now. When you admitted it."

"They heard everything!" He spoke in a rush. "I had no choice!"

"No choice. I get it. Nobody would blame you. But now we have a problem. I still have your daughter. I still need you to deliver the engine designs. What sort of solution will work? How do we keep the government out of this?"

Elbows on the table, Lalande clasped his hands together and leaned his head against them. He'd walked into a trap. He wondered if Galeri's phone copy might provide hope.

"Well?" Monique said.

"There are...other ways."

"I see why they put you in charge. You know every angle. How do we make this work?"

"Well—"

"I have an idea."

"What?"

"Give the plans to Sam Raven. The government agents won't watch him. He hands over the plans and you get your daughter back. Clear?"

"I will tell him."

"He'll argue, of course. You better convince him."

"I will make him understand." The edge returned to Lalande's voice. It was all or nothing now. If Galeri's phone trick failed, he'd have no choice but to follow Monique's suggestion. He might have to sacrifice Raven in exchange for Monique.

He wondered if Raven would understand.

He wondered how he'd live with himself after.

But it was preferable to wondering how he'd live without Nicoline.

37

RAVEN TWISTED AROUND IN THE PASSENGER SEAT. "SUCCESS?"

Galeri furiously tapped his keyboard. "We got the phone and I'm trying to trace the video feed. Almost there."

Cord announced, "She's getting up."

"Dammit!" Galeri said. "I need more—"

"She's moving," Cord said. He started the car.

"Stay with her," Raven said. "Ike?"

"Her signal is gone but I may have enough to work with."

Cord pulled into traffic as Monique slid into a cab. Raven phoned Lalande and told him to get back to the hotel—Raven's hotel, where they'd agreed to meet up after the operation. It made no sense to go all the way back to the Lalande estate. The CEO tried to talk further, but Raven cut him off. He'd noticed Monique left without the tablet. The doctored plans hadn't passed her test.

They needed to move *fast*. Raven had no intention of facing Noel and Alizee Lalande for failing to bring back Nicoline.

RAVEN TRIED NOT to focus on two things at once. He had one part of his mind on Monique's destination, and the other on Galeri's work in the back seat. The bearded man kept his head down and fingers busy. Raven didn't bother him with questions. Galeri would find the location of the video feed or he wouldn't.

Cord struggled with fast and slow traffic, but Raven told him to watch the road while he kept eyes on Monique's cab. He called out the turns and lane changes as they happened. She didn't go anywhere Raven wasn't already aware of. Ramon's apartment—a brief stop where she entered with only her purse and exited fifteen minutes later with her purse and a stuffed tote bag. She climbed back into the cab and the driver continued the trip.

Cord kept up but heavier traffic required both him and Raven to watch. Other cabs joined the flow and confused them.

"This is getting tricky," Cord said.

"Stay cool," Raven told him. "What do you have, Ike?"

"No exact location of the video feed, but I do have an area we can check."

"How big is the area?"

"I pinned it within a ten-mile radius."

Cord laughed. "Bet you're sorry you asked."

"Doesn't matter," Raven said. "We'll find it. Forget Monique, we gotta move on the video location. She didn't take the plans. Lalande will have to do something else and in the meantime, they'll move the girl. We have to get there before they do."

"The hotel?" Cord asked. "He's in your room by now."

Raven checked his watch and agreed with Cord. "Yeah, let's go. We'll see what the phone delivers and go from there."

Cord changed lanes to make a left turn ahead.

Raven wondered if he made the right call.

MONIQUE WORE a tight grimace as her cab driver headed for Broularid's home. She wanted to ask her boss for an alternative location to take Nicoline Lalande. She welcomed Ramon's help and appreciated his effort, but she wanted the girl out of the warehouse ASAP. If any of the thugs stepped out of line, they'd place everything at risk. Nicoline could *not* be mistreated if they wanted her father to cooperate. And there was still Sam Raven to consider. If they remained in one place too long, he might find them. If he did, she wanted Broularid's men to deal with him, not two-for-a-quarter (actually, ninety-five cents after inflation) thugs.

The cab was quiet, but rode a little rough over the Paris streets. Monique stared out the window and forced her facial muscles to relax. The tightness faded.

She could huff and puff all she wanted, but deep down, Monique only wanted to keep Nicoline Lalande away from men who fancied themselves a future big shot gang leader. Men like Monique's father. Committing or ordering a murder was one thing; allowing another woman to be violated crossed an invisible line she didn't see any reason to defend. She'd made up her mind; no discussion sought or required.

When she arrived at Broularid's, the butler showed her to the upstairs balcony. Paris sprawled in the distance; the breeze carried with it the sounds of the busy city.

"You caught me at a good time."

Monique turned from the balcony as Broularid stepped onto the patio. He gestured to a nearby table and they sat. The butler brought coffee. She turned her nose up at the thought of another cup so soon. Broularid told her to talk while he added cream and sugar and Monique ignored her cup.

She explained the situation at the warehouse but spun it as if her primary concern was using outside help who might somehow leak information. If one person talked, another would talk, and soon Sam Raven would be knocking on their door.

"It's possible," Broularid said. "I do appreciate Ramon trying to help. Do you have another place in mind?"

"I was thinking a hotel room somewhere in the city."

"A public place? Why?"

She informed Broularid of Raven's two rules, which she'd learned via further research into his background.

"He may still—"

"He will," she said. "And when he hesitates, we'll have him."

"Has Raven been known to break these rules?"

"He's more known for trying to steer opposition onto a more favorable battleground."

"You expect he'll deliver the plans the way you and Lalande discussed?"

"This is the beauty of the plan. We get everything we want, including Raven's head, and Lalande is left without his champion."

"Under the circumstances, do you think Raven will take a chance on a public fight?"

"He's alone. If he had help, maybe; certainly, he won't risk the Lalande girl. Getting her back alive trumps everything."

"Okay. I'll assign our people for security. Tell Ramon he and his friend will be compensated but we will no longer need their assistance."

"I need at least three men to help move the girl. We need to keep the other crew in the dark."

"Fine. Drink your coffee, my dear. By the time you finish, your armed escorts will be here."

The coffee was cold by the time she took a sip.

38

NOEL LALANDE PACED ACROSS THE HOTEL ROOM. HE SHOOK with nervous energy. The Galeri phone remained untouched in his jacket; the jacket hung on the back of a chair.

Where was Raven? Had something happened? What would he do without Raven's input?

Stop. You're too emotional. We've never reacted to a crisis like this before.

We've never been in a crisis like this before!

They're using my child as a bargaining chip. My child! How am I supposed to react?

Lelande stopped mid-pace and pivoted to face the door. The electronic lock clicked and the door swung inward. Raven entered first. Galeri and Cord followed.

Lalande straightened his back and nodded. "I was beginning to think you ran into trouble."

The door swung shut behind the three men.

"No," Raven said. "We might have a lead on where your daughter is, thanks to the video feed Monique showed you."

"It worked?" Lalande raised an eyebrow.

"We got it," Raven said.

Lalande sighed with relief.

Galeri set up the laptop on the desk against the forward wall. Lalande retrieved the cloned phone and Galeri plugged it into the laptop via a USB cable.

Raven looked over Galeri's shoulder. The list of contacts and associated numbers meant little. Galeri admitted it might take a while to trace each number, but Raven planned to bundle up the data and send it to Clark Wilson at the CIA. Wilson and his experts would dig up who belonged to which number very quickly.

Galeri next displayed the ten-mile circle within which the streaming video of Nicoline originated. This time, Lalande took a closer look.

"What are you looking at?" Lalande asked. "I only see a circle around a cluster of buildings and part of the river."

"We know she's not in the river," Cord quipped. He ignored Raven's raised eyebrow.

Lalande's attention never left the laptop screen. "Do we have to search this whole area? We need more men!"

Galeri took over. "We have warehouses, these apartment buildings, and row of retail shops—"

Lalande grabbed Raven's arm. The room's air conditioner hummed in the background, but beads of sweat coated the CEO's forehead. "We can't rule out any of them. They might have her in an apartment—"

"They might," Raven agreed.

He understood the older man's sense of urgency, and his pain, but the only solution was to go through the process, which meant work, which meant time. They didn't have a lot of time, but they had to use what few minutes were allotted to make the best call: the one that brought Nicoline home. There was no band-aid in the meantime.

A chime sounded from the clone phone. Raven asked Lalande to bring the device to him. Lalande retrieved it from the pocket of his coat and handed it over. A red dot appeared in the upper right corner near the battery life indicator. Raven asked Galeri what the indication meant.

"She's using her phone."

"Can we listen?"

"Once the red dot goes away. We can't listen as she's talking because the data is collecting."

Raven didn't quite understand, but Galeri was the expert. The bearded man turned his attention back to the laptop. Raven and Lalande stared at the red dot like a pair of anxious cats. The light finally switched off after a few minutes.

"Now what, Ike?"

Galeri grabbed the phone from Raven, tapped the screen to open a program, and tapped again on a lone MP3 file displayed in a folder. After activating the speaker function, he gave the phone back to Raven.

"It's me." Monique.

"What is it? Why aren't you back yet?" A man. Raven frowned. Ramon Crozier?

"We're moving the girl. I want out of that stinking warehouse."

"Monique—"

"I'm on my way with some guys Broularid assigned. I have a new place picked out, and, no, I'm not telling you yet. I don't want your friends to overhear."

"I'm alone, they can't hear. When do you expect to get back?"

"We'll be there as soon as possible. Traffic is horrible."

"Okay. I won't tell them we're moving her."

"See you soon."

They said good-bye and the call ended.

Raven said to Ike, "Which warehouse?"

"This one, the one on the left," Galeri said, pressing a stubby left index finger onto the laptop screen. "It's not associated with any company right now. The one next to it is part of a grocery chain. I doubt Nicoline is there."

Raven said, "We gotta move. Now."

Cord headed for the door as Galeri stood, leaving the computer on the desk. Raven turned to Lalande. "Stay here. We'll be back."

"By myself? What do I tell my wife?" Lalande blocked Raven's route to the door.

"Now? Nothing. I don't want to get her hopes up."

"What do you mean?"

Raven moved around the older man and headed for the door. Cord held it open.

"Answer me!"

Raven, Galeri, and Cord marched out like soldiers without second thoughts. The door shut with finality.

"Raven!" Lalande shouted. But he knew better than to charge out to the hall and make a scene.

"DID you hear the name she mentioned?" Raven said. "Broularid. Mean anything to you?"

Raven sat in the passenger seat while Galeri drove. Cord had the back seat. Galeri knew the area they were going to better so it made sense for him to drive. Traffic was thick but not as bad as rush hour—it was the lunch rush. Galeri had no choice but to drive under the limit. There was no room to go faster.

"Broularid," Galeri repeated. "Bit of a recluse. Big money man. Investor, all that."

"Is he dirty?"

"Not that I've ever heard, but if he's giving Monique men to move a kidnap victim—"

Cord said, "He's your mastermind. Bet on it."

"I'll tell Wilson about him, and the numbers on Monique's phone, after we get Nicoline back."

"At least we still have daylight," Galeri said.

Galeri braked as the brake lights on the car ahead flared. Galeri switched to the left lane when a space opened and sped around the slowing car. A bus ahead slowed traffic further. Galeri let out a curse.

"I'm going to have to break a rule if there's other people around when we get there," Raven said. "We gotta play this right. I don't want anybody getting hurt who doesn't deserve it. Cord, what do you have in the trunk?"

"Beretta pistol, and an old Uzi I picked up."

"Don't go nuts with full-auto," Raven said.

"What if *they* go nuts?"

Raven let out a frustrated breath. "This is why I work by certain standards, and I hate breaking them."

"What about Monique?" Cord asked. "If we get a shot—"

"Take it," Raven said. "I don't care who gets her. The goal is Nicoline."

"Copy that," Cord said. Galeri mumbled his own acknowledgement.

Raven's trigger finger was itchy, but if he was going to allow an engagement in public where innocent people might be hurt, he had to shoot true. There was no room for error. And they had to make sure the bad guys had as little chance to shoot back as possible.

He took a deep breath. He was gambling, and the stakes were higher than he would have liked. He was playing with lives.

39

GALERI FOLLOWED THE ROADWAY ALONG THE SEINE UNTIL HE came to a left turn. He made the turn through the intersection with only a light screech of the Peugeot's thin tires. Two blocks to go. They passed shops on one side and apartments on the other. Galeri cruised by the target warehouse. Raven counted two cars out front. Cord spotted two men loitering in the back. Both wore sunglasses and waist-length coats.

"Easy to hide weapons with those," Raven noted.

Galeri drove another block, made a right, and drove one more block before parking on the street. He left the motor running. He said, "What do you think?"

Raven examined the densely-packed buildings around them. The rough streets. Cars parked curbside. Heavy street traffic. Sporadic pedestrians. Broad daylight. They had to hit the warehouse with small arms in the middle of the day, and the traffic level didn't help. They'd hit a jam on escape. If any of the enemy survived to pursue, the gun fight would spread to the middle of whatever street on which they found themselves.

"Dammit," Raven said.

"We don't even know she's in there for sure," Cord said, leaning forward. "We go charging in blasting and it might be embarrassing."

"Only Embarrassing?" Galeri said.

"Ike?" Raven said. "Keep the car running. Cord, with me."

Raven opened his door and stepped out. Cord pulled down one portion of the back seat, grabbed a tote bag from the trunk, and took out a Beretta 92FS and a spare magazine. He joined Raven on the sidewalk with his pistol in his belt and the spare mag in a pocket. Raven started walking.

At the end of the block, they remained beside a building wall and watched the rear of the warehouse across the street. Large and rectangular, made of red brick with metal sliding doors spaced out along the back wall. The two men loitering at the rear had the parking lot to themselves; the two cars Raven spotted were parked up front, at odd angles, as if the drivers had hurriedly stopped because they didn't intend to stay long. Did the cars belong to Monique and the gun crew en route, or to the gunners currently inside?

Raven said nothing to Cord. He started for the crosswalk and Cord followed. They followed the sidewalk past the warehouse, all brick and dirty windows, to the front. Raven peeked around the corner at the two cars.

"What's on your mind?" Cord said.

"Are we early or late?"

"If we were early, they'd be on their way out," Cord said. "I don't think Monique is one to sit and chatter, especially if she doesn't like it here."

"And if we're late?"

"Maybe she'll make another phone call."

"Let's go to the rear again," Raven said. "I want to see what those guys have under their coats. They've been out too long for a smoke break."

"And brick walls stop bullets, you know," Cord said. He followed Raven back the way they'd come.

"You noticed, too? How's your French?"

"Perfect."

"Follow my lead."

Raven took out his phone to call Galeri. He told him to bring the car closer. They were going in.

RAVEN AND CORD turned the corner and walked into the rear parking lot of the warehouse. The two men at the rear door noticed them immediately, but issued no challenge with 20 yards still between them. Raven started talking in French. With animated gestures, he told a joke about what the baguette cried as the chef started slicing.

"Ouch! Le pain!"

Cord laughed. Ten yards. One of the two men ahead cracked a smile, but his partner did not. The partner raised a hand.

"This is private property."

Raven brought his raised right hand down in a sharp chop, catching the man in the side of the throat. He followed up with a left hook into the man's gut. The man doubled over.

His partner grabbed for something dangling under his coat. The suppressor-fitted snout of a Russian-made Veresk SR-2 submachine gun nosed its way to Cord as the American moved closer. Beretta in hand, Cord slammed the Italian steel into the side of the man's head. He dropped. Cord stowed the pistol and reached for the sub gun.

Raven kicked the first man in the head, knocking him unconscious. He, too, grabbed the SR-2 under the man's coat. He helped himself to a spare mag. A sound suppressor extended the SR-2's muzzle same as Cord's.

A horn tooted behind them. Raven looked. Galeri had the Peugeot stopped at the end of the lot. Raven waved. Cord tried to rear door. It eased open under his slow pull. The brightness outside made it look dark inside; Cord slipped through the doorway, Raven behind him. Raven let the door close to a crack against the pressure of his hand. The catch didn't click.

THE ANGLED floor to their right met the sliding doors of the loading dock so it would be level with semi-trailers. No threats. Debris littered the cold concrete floor; a layer of dust showed scrapes where shoes had stepped or items dragged from point A to point B. On their left, rows of stacked pallets. And dim light from the dirty windows in the roof.

Bright light was concentrated on the other end, across the warehouse floor. And voices. Low-volume conversations indicated several occupied hostiles. They weren't expecting trouble. They believed they were insulated.

Not quite, guys, Raven thought.

Raven let his eyes adjust. He gestured left. Cord followed him to the rows of stacked pallets; splinter city, but good cover. For now.

"What's on your mind?" Cord whispered.

Raven looked through gaps in the stack.

"They got a section of empty shelving between here and the lights," he whispered back. "You go wide around to the far wall on the left, and I'll go through. When they focus on me, surprise 'em."

"Stay out of my muzzle sweep."

Raven scoffed. "Get going."

Cord left more scrapes in the floor dust as he shifted and moved further into the dark. Raven peered ahead. The rows of shelves nearly reached the roof. They were empty, metal skeletal frames with wooden planks at intervals to the top. As dusty as the floor.

But conversation continued in the lighted area.

Raven left the pallets with careful steps.

40

AT LEAST THE CAMERA WASN'T STARING AT HER ANY LONGER.

Nicoline Lalande's entire body was one big cramp. They'd tied her roughly to the chair, arms behind the back, ankles to the legs, and about all she might do to change her situation was fall to one side or the other. The chair was solid wood; a fall wouldn't break it and allow her freedom of movement. It was the kind of stunt that only happened in the movies anyway, she decided.

But if she had to sit with pain and a gag over her mouth, at least she hadn't been molested, attacked, raped, or otherwise humiliated, but the longer the woman who gave the orders not to hurt her remained gone, the more Nicoline wondered if the goons would ignore her. They played poker in the next room. They played poker loudly, seemingly uninterested in her once the video was sent, and it worked in her favor.

The only time they bothered her was to take her to the bathroom, and one guard always stood with her in the restroom. She had the stall to herself, but knowing there was a goon on the other side with a gun listening to her pee surprisingly made one unable to relieve themselves. If she couldn't during one break, she did on the next one; there was only so much the body could store and all that.

Sweat trickled down her neck. Along with the full-body cramp, she was wet all over, too, from sweating in a stuffy room. They gave her water after each bathroom break, but not as much as she wanted.

What was going on?

The men with the guns who stopped her father's car and pulled her out barely registered in her mind any longer. Had she already blocked them out? Would they come back, vividly, later on? Would she even survive the next 24 hours?

Nicoline tried not to panic. She was a Lalande, after all, and her father's daughter. If anybody had the connections and the friends to help free her, her father did. And who was the man with him in the car? The man with the gun he hadn't tried to hide from her view.

So many questions.

The commotion continued in the next room as somebody won a hand and they shuffled cards once again.

CORD IGNORED the left-side brick wall for two offices set in the back corner. A 90-degree wall showed two doors; Lounge and Quality Assurance, according to the slip-signs mounted above eye-level. The door to QA was closed. The door to the lounge was partially open, darkness beyond the gap.

Cord slid onto his belly to stay out of sight. The dust almost made him cough. He examined the lounge door.

If I push on that door, it'll squeak, he thought. *And if I don't, we'll learn the hard way there are gunners sleeping in there and they'll be up our backside.*

He had to investigate.

Carefully.

Cord eased to his feet. The shelving and low light helped conceal him, but a gunfight with such a large open area, devoid of close cover, wasn't his idea of a good time. There was going to be a fight. He wanted the best advantage when it began.

He approached the half-open door. Stopping at the wall, he tried to see inside. At least there was no snoring or other noises. The visible clutter confirmed no threat, and he doubted anybody had gone inside in quite some time. A foul odor emanated. Something had died in there. A rat, maybe. More than one rat, probably. He wanted out of there. Cord turned and followed the 90-degree wall to the corner, and remained close as he made his way to the brick wall ahead.

The continuing chatter of the hostiles told him he and Raven remained undetected.

RAVEN REACHED THE SHELVES. The voices were louder. He translated as they spoke. They had a poker game going, and covered several topics, but nobody talked about a hostage.

Until:

"Who's turn is it to take the girl for a pee break?"

Bingo.

Men grumbled and then one volunteered.

"You just like to watch," said another, to a chorus of laughter.

Raven dropped low. He waited. A wide hall ahead opened to a narrower one going left to right; the light was concentrated in the narrow hall. More commotion. Sharp commands from a male, answered by insults and protests from a female. Presently the pair crossed the gap of the wide hall. The man held his sub gun in his left hand, and clutched one of Nicoline Lalande's arms with the other. She struggled against the grasp but the man held firm. They disappeared down the other end of the hall. A door squeaked and closed with a thud.

Now!

"Cord!" Raven hissed, hoping his partner saw the situation same as him. Raven rose and trotted across the concrete to the wide hall, letting the resumed poker game cover him. A shadow on his left became Cord as the freelancer entered the light. He stayed on the left wall; Raven the right. Raven gestured toward the bathroom. Cord nodded.

Raven peeked around the corner; clear. The voices came from an open doorway ten feet from him. Raven eased around the corner and approached. Reaching the doorway, he finally heard the slap and shuffle of cards.

He swung through the doorway with the SR-2 sub gun at his shoulder. Three men sat at a circular table; money, loose cards, and cigarettes cluttered the tabletop. One man stood watching, and held his weapon casually.

The man on his feet looked to the doorway expecting to see his comrade after the bathroom trip. He saw Raven instead, and let out a "Ugh!" as he tried to get his SR-2 into action. It was the last sound he made as a living creature.

Raven fired a three-round burst. The 9x21mm bullet, designed to defeat body armor, ripped into the standing man's chest. Only the rapid thumps of rounds leaving the suppressed muzzle and the clicking of the weapon's action made any noise; the suppressor did its job well. The nipple-tipped slugs continued out the man's back, trailing pieces of flesh and flecks of blood. The bigger pool of red grew beneath him after he fell.

Raven shifted targets and blasted the card shuffler sitting alone on the left side of the table. His sights next settled on one of the remaining two. The burst knocked the man out of his chair, and as the dead man crashed to the floor, the last crawled under the table and tipped it over. The items atop the table clattered onto the floor, but the fellow either didn't realize the futility of using thin sheet metal against armor-piercing bullets, or reacted out of desperation.

The snout of the last man's SR-2 appeared over the top. Raven shifted out of the doorway as the wild burst of auto fire chewed into the doorframe and beyond. Raven swung back, low this time, and let his SR-2 spit on full auto. The 9x21 projectiles shredded the tabletop and punched into the meat target behind. The man screamed. Raven reloaded and entered the room. Stepping over a body to the other side of the table, he fired another burst into the last man to make sure he never got up.

Raven reached the hallway again as the bathroom door squeaked open.

41

THE BATHROOM ESCORT WASN'T AS SLOW AS HIS BUDDIES, Raven noticed.

He exited with Nicoline in front of him, holding her by the left shoulder, the snout of his Veresk SR-2 jammed into her back. He had to hunch to keep his head below her shoulders.

Raven lifted his SR-2 to eye-level. "Let her go!"

"Put the gun down or I'll kill her!"

Raven's eyes darted to Cord, who remained around the corner where Raven had left him. Cord lowered himself to the floor and approached the corner on his belly.

Raven kept talking.

"Your buddies are dead. You can walk away. Let her go and I will give you a head start."

"Liar!"

"Which part?"

The gunner said, "Huh?" as Cord cleared the corner. From his level on the floor, he had a shot, but not one to guarantee a kill. The gunner still might have enough time to fire into Nicoline's back.

Raven's pulse jumped.

Cord fired. His slug slapped into the flesh of the gunner's stomach. The man opened his mouth to gasp, his grip on Nicoline's shoulder loosening...

Nicoline dived to the floor. As soon as her move exposed the gunner, Raven and Cord fired again and again. The gunner's clothes turned red from the impacts. He fell before Nicoline had a chance to look back. But she didn't look back. She turned her wide eyes on Raven and screamed.

NICOLINE'S SCREAM cut off sharply once Raven helped her stand. She stared at him with wide eyes and a sweaty face; she blurted, "You're the one who was with my father!"

"We're taking you to him. Can you run?"

"I'll run forever if it gets me out of here."

"Let's go. Lead the way, Cord!"

The trio raced across the warehouse floor for the rear door. Cord exited first and waved to Galeri, still waiting in the Peugeot. Galeri hit the gas and chirped the tires entering the parking lot, but met Raven, Cord, and Nicoline halfway. The three piled inside. Galeri spun the car around and drove away. Raven glanced around the street. The suppressed weapons had kept the fight quiet; nobody had noticed. A good thing. The only people dead were the ones who deserved to be.

The four remained silent while Galeri made several turns and drove along the back streets to put space between them and the warehouse battleground. Nicoline, in the back with Raven, took time to catch her breath. Raven handed her a handkerchief to wipe her face. She did so, and leaned back in the seat.

"What's this about? Why did this happen?" she finally asked.

Raven told her. This was no time to hold back. Doing so would only make her more upset. When he finished, she instead seemed more confused.

"I don't get it."

"Your father will explain more. You'll see him soon."

"Are you taking me to the house?"

"My hotel," Raven said. "He's waiting there. And he's the reason we found you. Your Pop is a brave man."

"I know," she said, and turned to look out the window. With her glazed expression, and unblinking stare, Raven wondered if she truly saw any of the passing scenery.

Raven finally let out a breath of his own. He watched Galeri drive; Cord sat beside Ike, but kept to himself.

They'd been lucky.

Raven hoped their luck held. Monique and her crew, and the mysterious "Broularid", weren't going to give up and run away. Their scheme was known to the Lalandes; Raven himself remained a threat; if anything, the siren song of "kill 'em all" would soon bellow from the enemy camp.

Let them come.

With Nicoline out of the free fire zone, Raven wanted the enemy in front of his gun *very* much. He welcomed the next engagement.

———————

FATHER AND DAUGHTER embraced with grateful tears, Nicoline having run into her father's embrace before Raven and the other two men made it through the doorway.

Raven let them have their moment. He told Galeri to get back on the laptop and find the name named Broularid. He wanted to call Clark Wilson in the US and get him going on the numbers in Monique's phone.

"What do I do?" Cord asked.

"Take a load off."

Cord didn't argue. He stretched out on the bed to nap.

While Galeri's fingers worked the laptop and Lalande and his daughter huddled in a chair (she was on his lap, head buried against a shoulder), Raven grabbed the cloned phone from beside the laptop and found a corner to stand while he called the CIA.

Wilson didn't answer, but one of his team picked up instead. He was an analyst named Heinrich. Wilson, the analyst said, needed a day off.

"Don't we all," Raven said. "I have a list of numbers I want to send you. I'm looking for one person in particular, but there might be another corresponding with whoever the leak is at your end—"

Raven explained Monique's mention of Broularid and his desire to know where the man might be found. "I know he's in Paris, but not where."

"Send 'em over," Heinrich said. "We'll get on it."

"Is Clark's email all right, or should I use yours?"

"Send to Clark. I have access and you have it memorized."

"On the way."

Raven next called Roger Justice in San Francisco to check on Kayla. Roger answered with a quiet hello.

"You in a museum or something?" Raven said.

"Kayla and Lia are sleeping. I'm on watch."

"How is she?"

"Lia's fabulous."

"Roger—"

"I'm kidding, boss. Kayla is doing good, but doesn't like being cooped up. She says we're her friendly prison guards.

But she's doing all right otherwise. Her FBI buddies are taking care of things."

"Any ID on the shooters?"

"All three came from France, all with extensive criminal records. They entered the US on false passports. FBI is trying to trace where they found their weapons, but I expect it will be a local source with no connection."

"DO they know who those shooters might be connected with in Paris?"

"Not that I'm aware of."

"Doesn't matter unless some leads we have now don't pan out," Raven said, "and I expect they will."

"Want me to wake Kayla?"

"Let her sleep. Tell her I called. She'll be mad you didn't get her, but say I overruled you."

"Copy that. Anything else?"

"Not now. Thank you, Roger."

"Of course."

Raven put his phone away and glanced at the cloned phone. The contact list had gone through without difficulty. Heinrich and his colleagues at CIA would go through the list fast. Soon, he'd have the answers he needed.

He went over to Lalande and his daughter. Nicoline shifted away from her father so she could see him. The CEO said, "I can't thank you enough."

"You need to get your wife and daughter out of Paris as soon as you can."

"There is still a threat?"

"For sure," Raven said. "Do you have somewhere you can go nobody knows about? Not a vacation home, nothing on record."

He frowned, shook his head.

"Daddy, what about—"

She didn't finish her question. Her father picked up right

away and snapped his finger. "Yes. It will be fine." To Raven: "Do you need us to keep in touch with you?"

"Keep your phone handy. I'll call you when it's over. Or you'll know when it's over if I don't make it."

"What do you mean?"

"Trust me. You'll know."

Galeri announced, "Got a hit on Broularid, Raven."

Sonner than I thought.

Raven excused himself and joined Galeri at the desk.

42

AT CIA HEADQUARTERS, IN THE OFFICES OF SPECIAL
Activities, analyst Paul Heinrich and his crew broke Monique
Choffron's cell phone contact list into groups and spread the
workload around the department. Wilson had briefed Heinrich on the importance of the project, the national security
threat, and the number of murders so far.

Tracing the phone numbers and identifying who they
belonged to wasn't tough. Monique included either first
names or nicknames on her list, which helped match the real
people, all of whom showed up in either CIA or Interpol
files. All of her associates were crooks. If Monique had a
particular hair dresser or friend not involved in criminal
activity, they weren't on the list.

Heinrich took the big task, the effort to trace the man
named Broularid. Once he identified the man's number, a
quick background check revealed publicly-know business
and family history, and details of what happened to his wife
and daughter while on a humanitarian mission during the
Balkan War.

Heinrich then went a step further. He pinged Broularid's

cell. The computer pinpointed the phone's location at a chateau outside Paris. A check on the address confirmed Broularid owned the chateau and had done so outright for at least two decades. Next, he needed to find a way to hack the phone and extract the man's own call history. If he'd spoken to his source at the Agency, Heinrich could link the two together. To accomplish the goal, he needed to get in touch with the technical services department in another part of the building. Technical services included the CIA's "white hat" hackers. If an item had a microchip and a processor, the team could break into it, dig up any secrets, and deliver the requested information.

Heinrich emailed Broularid's number, location, and background to the tech section, and marked his request *urgent*. Then he went for coffee.

RAVEN TOOK a cab to Broularid's chateau and told the uninterested driver to let him out in front of the gate. As soon as he exited the car, the guard in the gate shack had an eye on him, and spoke into a hand-held radio. The cab driver agreed to wait, and parked on the side of the road. Raven tapped on the plastic window of the guard shack. The guard, shorter than Raven, stepped out.

"This is private property," the guard said. He wore no sidearm.

"I'm here to see Pierre Broularid. Tell him Sam Raven is here."

The guard returned to the shack and used the radio again. A flurry of conversation, repeated requests, and an argument ended when the guard hit a switch to open the gate and told Raven to walk to the front porch. Somebody would greet him there.

Raven stayed to the side of the long driveway as it wound its way to the big house. Groundskeepers looked busy; they watched him, too. Raven assumed they had easy access to more than simple garden tools if a sudden situation arose.

Either that, or they wondered why he wasn't in a car like every other visitor to the place.

When he reached the front door, nobody waited for him. *Typical.* He rang the bell.

A butler answered the door. The man wore the requisite black uniform with a full head of gray hair. He frowned at Raven sand said nothing. Unlike the guard at the gate, he was taller than Raven, and peered along the edge of his nose as he sized up the surprise guest.

"Sam Raven to see Pierre Broulard."

The butler opened the door wider, stepping back and gesturing for Raven to enter. Raven walked inside. He wore his gun under his jacket, and had a second surprise in the right pocket of the jacket, but the butler didn't frisk him. Nor did anybody else show up to pat him down. If he'd passed through a concealed X-ray in the doorway, nobody seemed to care.

The butler finally said, "Please follow me," and led Raven down a wood-paneled hallway to a library. Books lined the walls, leather furniture throughout; a corner seat appeared well-worn. All the room lacked was a burning fire place. A bar on one wall contained the required brandy, however.

"The master of the house will be with you shortly." The butler departed, closing the door quietly behind him.

Raven dropped into the well-worn leather seat. It was soft and comfortable and agreed with him. When the door next opened, he'd be covered briefly, and have a second or two to react first if the Frenchman didn't enter alone.

He sat in the silent room for five minutes. Nothing made

any noise within, except Raven as he breathed. Broularid wanted a library; he had one.

Raven wondered why he hadn't been searched. They knew he was the enemy. He had not shown up for a fight, though. He had a different goal in mind. HE wanted a moment with the mastermind, to get a look at the man up close, finally see whom he was up against. But if Broularid wanted action, Raven would put an end to the shenanigans fast.

The door opened. The man who entered looked older than the most recent news photo showed. He wore a sweater and slack combo and Raven expected him to launch into the French equivalent of "won't you be my neighbor". The man shut the door, then noticed Raven in the corner seat.

"I suppose you could have ambushed me, Mr. Raven."

"No." Raven stood. Reluctantly. "Chair's too comfortable. Also, a fight isn't he reason for my visit."

"Which I figured. And it's also why we allowed you to enter with a weapon. Care for a drink?"

Broularid crossed to the small bar.

"I'll pass."

"Understandable. At least have a seat, please. You're making me feel like a poor host."

Raven picked one of the couches in the center of the room. Broularid fixed his drink and then sat opposite. The table between them provided a buffer, but not enough to protect the Frenchman from what Raven carried inside his jacket pocket.

The Frenchman spoke.

"It's a shame we aren't on the same side. We both want the same thing. Can we agree there is too much violence in the world, and innocent people suffer more than the perpetrators? Especially when the perpetrators are governments who are certain they're doing the right thing?"

"I wouldn't go any further," Raven said.

Broularid let out a laugh. "Mr. Raven, please. Your argument with me concerns the deaths of your friends. I'm sorry. What happened with David and Jen was regrettable. I did not make the decision regarding the Lalande family casually, either. We both use violence to achieve our goals, but only when we must, and there is no other choice. Maybe you've convinced yourself it's okay for you, but not for me, and I must disagree with you."

Raven said nothing.

"You imagine we're different, Mr. Raven. We are not. We've both suffered as innocent parties. We are both reacting in ways natural to us. And if it means anything, you've killed *far* more people than I."

"So you're better, and I'm worse?"

"The people working for me, and *with* me, believe in our cause. The Denoshas became an exception. A rare occurrence, I assure you."

"Am I supposed to feel better now?"

Broularid sipped his drink, but Raven saw him crack. He wasn't getting through and knew Raven recognized his rambling line of bullshit. But he was going to keep trying. The Frenchman said, "What are you here for, Mr. Raven?"

"I hope you'll listen to reason. I get Jen and Dave were part of your plan, and they aren't here to tell me why. I'm willing to call off my vendetta regarding them."

"In exchange for what?"

"You leave the Lalande family alone. You work only with those who have already joined you. No more recruitments or threats. Or kidnappings. Keep it in the family, if you know what I mean."

"Mr. Raven—"

"And I want the name of your contact at the CIA."

Broularid laughed again. "Are you serious? My goodness, you are indeed. What you are asking for—"

"Is a small price to pay to die an old man."

"I'm already an old man."

"Of natural causes, then."

"I get to die in bed, is that what you're telling me?"

"Wear boots if you'd like."

"This is out of character for you, Mr. Raven. I'm, frankly, stunned."

"No, it's perfectly in character. Once we identified you, I had to see for myself who you were, if you were truly the man we're looking for, all that noise. You think I'm going to come blasting in here and kill everything that moves without confirmation?"

Broularid offered half a grin in reply.

"But I can do that, if you want," Raven added. He finally extracted the item he carried in his jacket. He showed Broularid an M67 fragmentation grenade provided by Ike Galeri. He pulled the pin; metal scratched metal as the pin left the housing, and within seconds the only thing keeping the M67 from detonating was the pressure of Raven's grip. The baseball-type grenade contained 6.5 ounces of composition B explosive, which didn't seem like much. But the M67 had a *fatal radius* of sixteen feet. Letting the grenade go in the confines of the library would kill them both and, worse, destroy most of the books lining the walls.

Color drained from Broularid's face, but he kept his composure.

"Maybe we *should* have searched you," the Frenchman said.

"I want the Lalandes to remain unharmed, and no other defense personnel contacted. We all make choices. Dave and Jen made theirs. It was a poor choice, but they aren't the victims I thought they were. I asked myself what I was trying to avenge. Wasted youth, maybe. But it doesn't make a whole lot of sense considering Dave's lies and attempt to cover his ass. For an old pal, he had no trouble lying to me; then again, maybe I was fooling myself after everything that happened between him and me and Jen. But with the Lalandes I have a bigger reason to be here."

"You won't kill yourself *and* me, Mr. Raven. Put the pin back in and put the grenade away."

"It has to end sometime, Mr. Broularid. The war has gone on long enough. When the simple answers don't work anymore, you have to ask deeper questions."

"No. You won't do it. You came here to make a deal—"

Raven's eyes didn't leave the Frenchman's. Raven didn't have to speak to communicate. Broularid shifted in his seat.

"What if I say no?" the Frenchman asked.

Raven smiled. "Then this grenade assures I walk out of here. Our conflict will then follow its natural conclusion."

Broularid sighed with what appeared to be relief. "I'd rather we took such a course. You see, I am not alone in implementing my vision. My associates depend on secrecy, the ability to work for peace in our own way, undetected. If I allow the Lalandes, who know everything, to continue their existence, my associates will lose confidence in my leadership. Do you understand?"

"You left me out of your equation," Raven said.

"My counterproposal is as follows," Broularid continued. "You walk away. I do what's necessary to keep my organization safe, then restrict my activities as per your original suggestion. And I will *not* provide the name of my CIA contact. He is important. Ah, I see. Don't answer, Mr. Raven. You have the word *no* written across your face."

Raven inserted the pin back into the grenade. The metal scraped again. He gave the pin an extra push to make sure it seated. He was smiling.

"Why are you amused, Mr. Raven?"

Raven returned the grenade to his jacket, and met the Frenchman's eyes once again.

"I was right about you. When this conversation started, you tried to sell me the idea we were the same. You tried to convince me the only deaths you perpetrated were necessary and brought about by two people who got cold feet. No. You're a killer like the rest of them, we're quite opposite, and now we'll finish this the way we were meant to."

"I can order my men to shoot you. If you think you can get out of here alive—"

Raven stood. "Haven't you been paying attention? I've killed every man you've thrown at me, and next I'll kill the woman you hold in such high regard. I'll kill *you* last."

Raven turned for the door. When he opened it, he found the butler waiting.

Broularid called out, "Escort Mr. Raven outside. No harm is to come to him."

Raven turned back. "Until next time."

Broularid didn't leave his seat. He raised his glass instead. "Until the *last* time. Good luck, Mr. Raven."

Raven followed the silent butler to the front door. He kept an eye out for any tricks as he retraced his steps along the driveway, under the eyes of the groundskeepers, to the front gate. The cab driver remained in place as promised. Raven climbed into the back and told the driver to return to the city.

Raven reached inside his jacket to the pocket on the left. He pulled out a digital recorder, stopped it, and ran the audio back to the beginning of the meeting. Broularid's words replayed on the small speaker loud and clear. He pressed the stop button.

He and Cord and Galeri already had a plan.

Time to put it into action.

43

THE MEETING THAT TOOK PLACE AT THE LALANDE ESTATE
prior to Raven's visit to Broularid had been loud and vocal.
Brunelle, the French federal agent in charge of the Nicoline
case, was specifically upset with Raven for charging ahead
without advising them, as well as sending potentially important evidence, Monique's phone, to the Americans. Raven
only shrugged. Who else was he going to send to?

Before the pair exploded into a louder argument, Lalande
stepped in to calm the situation. They continued with the
conversation. Raven promised to hand over the phone to
Brunelle, and the federal agent refused to let Raven murder
more people on French soil. Broularid was too big a prize to
leave lying in the street. Broularid, he argued, needed to
stand trial before a French court, and answer for his crimes
with a prison sentence, not Raven's "vigilante justice". Raven
agreed, as long as Brunelle's attitude didn't extend to
Monique Choffron. Brunelle agreed to let Raven have the
woman while he got Broularid and the phone.

Raven also handed the voice recorder to Agent Brunelle.
The admission of guilt from the big man himself would aid

the French federal offices; meantime, they began building as much of a case as they could based on witness statements from Nicoline Lalande; Monique had mentioned the man's name in her presence, while arguing with her boyfriend. The kidnapping case was the strongest element they had to start with. Broularid openly admitted to organizing the abduction, and Nicoline promised to tell everything she saw, heard, witnessed; all of it. She showed her father's strength and will to push beyond hardship.

Killing the old man would have been too easy. Now he'd rot in prison for the rest of his natural life, and his crimes exposed. There'd be sympathy, of course; his intentions, while good, might have been carried out another way. But Raven knew the folly of man. It was easy to become blinded by a cause, or vision, and begin a course of action that seemed right, while missing fatal flaws. Sometimes the flaws only ended a trajectory from which one might recover and start again. This time, it ended in homicides, kidnapping, subversion. But Broularid still thought he was right.

As for his statements about David and Jen Denosha, Raven hadn't lied. The revelation occurred to him in the middle of the night before, around three a.m., when heart and mind are quiet and the truth can speak its piece. He wished they were alive to explain; he wished a lot of things. And while Jen was trying to set things right, she should have contributed more; let Raven protect her, instead of trying to escape and leave behind only bread crumbs with which to assemble the puzzle. Another decision that seemed right at the time.

In the end, his friends were the catalyst. Noel Lalande and his family were the true victims, and by the time he left France, Raven planned to see them protected from the threat posed by Broularid and his gang. Once and for all.

Raven's visit to Broularid, he and his associates finally decided, guaranteed two things.

One: Broularid would run, or fortify. No matter what he decided, French federal agents were watching his house.

Two: Broularid would warn Monique and her boyfriend, Ramon. They'd run and hide, hopefully somewhere outside the city. Raven and Brunelle didn't want civilian casualties.

At least, they were the two options Raven favored the most. He knew quite well the enemy might have a few surprises of their own.

———————

MONIQUE CHOFFRON and Ramon Crozier had been holed up in Ramon's apartment since the massacre (Monique had no other word for it) at the warehouse. Sam Raven showed no mercy; she wasn't surprised, but she also didn't know how to handle such a force. He had yet to be tested with Broularid's hand-picked gunners, but she didn't think they'd fare any better.

Ramon was talking on the phone. He was arguing with his buddy, Lucien, who had provided the warehouse and its security contingent. Broularid had warned Raven was on the attack. She and Ramon needed a place to hide, ASAP. They still had Broularid's men to count on, but she wanted a hideout not connected to the Source in any way. Ramon hoped Lucien might be willing to help a second time.

"We'll pay whatever you ask, in advance," Ramon said into the phone. He paced in the kitchen while Monique paced in the living room. She wanted to sit on the couch. She wanted to relax. But knowing a shark was swimming in her direction, teeth barred, looking to devour anything in its path, removed any chance of her nerves settling until she was sure they were safe.

"We have our own shooters," Ramon continued. "Unless you want to supply a few to get even with what happened to the warehouse crew. Yes, we expect he'll come for us. We don't know when. We want to be somewhere hard to find. I know I can count on you, Lucien, what do you say?"

Monique almost held her breath. She reminded herself to breath. *Slow. Don't panic. If this falls through we have other options.*

She hoped.

Ramon didn't speak for a few moments. Monique fought the urge to chew on her bottom lip or a nail. School girls did those things, not mature adults who should know how to handle stress. Where was a glass of wine when she needed one?

"All right," Ramon said. "Thank you, Lucien. I know exactly where it is, and we'll meet your men there in an hour or so."

She went to the kitchen with a hopefully look on her face.

Ramon smiled at her. "He said okay."

"To what?"

"A hideout in Versailles. Practically in a forest, lots of security, his men plus our men. The American won't dare attack us. He'll simply be overwhelmed and wiped out."

"Good." Monique's spirits brightened. She didn't know what Broularid was doing to stop Raven. He hadn't told her. All he'd said was to get out of town, somehow, and stay out of sight until he told her otherwise.

Neither took long to pack, and they were in Ramon's Mini and driving west.

Two cars followed them, both mixing into the traffic, alternating so Ramon didn't pick up the tail. As it was, he didn't bother checking. His attention was forward, out of Paris, to what he believed was safety, and driving as fast as he could to put distance between him, Monique, and the shark in pursuit.

44

RAVEN WAITED IN HIS HOTEL ROOM FOR IKE GALERI'S CALL.
Galeri was in one of the cars trailing Monique. A pair of
street toughs he'd recruited for the job rode in the other car,
with strict orders not to engage until Raven showed up at the
scene.

Raven lay on the bed, stretched out, hands behind his
head, contemplating the ceiling. Callen Cord sat at the desk
playing solitaire and losing several rounds, muttering curses;
Raven ignored him. He tried to run various scenarios
through his head. What if Monique did this, what if she did
that, how could he best react? The additional muscle Galeri
had brought along certainly helped, but how many guns
would they face in the final showdown? Galeri had at least
come through with plenty of firepower, which wasn't cheap,
and he couldn't provide Raven any price breaks. Raven had
paid the full amount via wire transfer. In case he didn't make
it back, he didn't want the supplier stuck without compensa-
tion. Besides, gun dealers weren't the kind of people one
wanted to piss off, dead or not.

Cord gathered up his playing cards and began to shuffle,

commenting, "Maybe if I give them an extra shuffle I'll play better."

Raven mumbled in reply. He continued picking out spots in the ceiling to stare at.

Time passed. The sky darkened outside, but neither man witnessed the change. The drapes remained closed across the window. It made the room feel smaller, almost like a coffin; if a sniper took a shot at them from the roof across the street, it might become a coffin for one of them. The drapes would cover the window for the duration.

When the cell phone on the nightstand rang, Cord's hands froze mid-deal; Raven reached for the phone. He tapped his thumb on the answer button and said, "What do you have, Ike?"

"I'm in Versailles. So is Monique, her boyfriend, and about fifteen men with automatic weapons. The gunmen arrived separately, and from here it looks like Ramon is in charge of whipping them into a unit."

"Where in Versailles?"

"Outside the city, but close enough you can be in town within twenty minutes. Mostly forest out here."

"Keep watch. Send me the location and Cord and I will get going."

"Got it. On the way." Raven ended the call.

Cord put the deck of cards back into the box. "What's the plan?"

"We'll take separate cars in case they're watching us. You leave first. If something happens, at least one of us will get there. Here are the directions." Raven left the bed and brought his phone to Cord, who wrote Galeri's note on a sheet of hotel stationary.

"What if they get us both?" Cord said.

"Then we're shit outta luck."

"Fair enough."

Raven and Cord slung on their pistol harnesses and Cord picked up a tote bag of other ordnance from near the door. He waved at Raven and departed without another word. Raven paced a little, checking his watch. He wanted to give Cord time to get away. Maybe ten minutes.

Raven took a moment to check the gear in his own tote bag. Galil ACE GEN II 7.62x39mm rifle with collapsible stock and red dot sight system. Six full magazines. Chest harness for the extra mags, and two M67 frag grenades. No body armor. Cord had chosen a chest plate for protection, but Raven never put much stock in bulletproof anything. He was either going to survive the fight or he wouldn't. His .45-caliber Nighthawk Custom Talon filled the shoulder holster under his left arm. Spare mags for the pistol rode under his right. He zipped up a jacket, and checked his watch again. Cord was long gone by now. He left the room and waited in the hallway till the door shut fully. Raven started for the elevator, walking casually, acting natural despite having a tote bag full of destructive hardware.

Another room door opened and shut. Two men behind Raven talked in low tones. Raven walked faster. He turned a corner into the elevator area and pressed the call button. None of the two doors opened. Raven waited. The other two men stood away from him, still talking. They weren't French. Raven recognized their language as Romanian. They were young, dark haired, trim, both wearing black jackets and jeans. Raven stepped further away. The jackets were zipped halfway, puffing out near the chest. He didn't spot any weapons but it didn't mean they weren't packing. And they might simply be fellow guests. Raven was well aware there were normal people staying at the hotel. Not everybody was out to kill him, but he'd stayed alive long enough by never expecting random people were benign.

The elevator to Raven's right dinged and the doors slid

open. Raven went inside. The two men followed. They stopped talking. Raven hit the button for the lobby. The doors slid shut.

Only the elevator's motor made any noise as the cabin descended. Then it slowed to a stop. The doors opened. Two more men entered. Nobody acknowledged each other. Raven leaned against the right wall, tote in his left hand in case he needed his .45. The door slid shut again. The descent continued.

Somebody said, "Raven."

One of the men moved toward him. Raven twisted left, bringing his right fist around and smacking the man in the face. He winced at the impact, but the man fell back, Raven dropping the tote as the other two more piled on and the third hit the stop switch. The elevator halted mid-floor.

Raven didn't bother to look where his fists went. He swung, he collided with the other bodies, felt the slam of their fists into his front and back. He crooked his right arm and fired his elbow back. An abrupt crunch told him he scored a hit. Somebody yelled. He punched the man in front of him, sent the opponent rolling away. Another hit from behind. Raven pivoted, hitting twice, then another slammed into his left side and shoved him into the wall. Raven clawed at the man's face, sinking a thumb into an eye socket. Another scream. The man withdrew. Raven dropped as another swung and hit the wall. Raven punched him in the balls. The other two piled on, grappling, striking, Raven hitting back. The elevator car shook and rattled as they struggled. Raven snapped his head back, felt the landing against a sharp chin, but the crack of teeth slamming together and a choked cry let him know he'd made contact. He sank a fist into the belly of the man in front of him, then grabbed his hair to hold his head up. One, two, three punches to the face. He let the man collapse onto the floor. He began to turn to face the last, but a kick to the back of his left leg sent him sprawling. He landed on top of one of the young fighters. Rolling onto his back, he met his attacker as he drew a knife and aimed for Raven's neck. Raven moved aside and the blade passed within an inch to plunge into the thigh of one of his partners. Raven clapped his hands over the man's ears, punched him in the nose, and as the man fell atop, rolled him aside and climbed to his feet.

Raven leaned against the wall, gasping, hurt, reeling from the blows, but he had to continue. He pulled one of the unconscious fighters away from his tote, picked up the bag, and hit the switch to start the elevator car moving again. He breathed hard, stood up, adjusted his jacket to better cover his pistol. He felt blood leaking on his face. He wiped the streak with a handkerchief, glancing at the red stain as he put the white cloth back in a pocket.

The doors opened on the lobby floor and a group of people stood waiting. Raven stepped out and walked fast. The waiting guests, with their luggage and impatient faces, gasped. Somebody screamed. Raven kept walking. He ignored curious looks and found the door to the under-ground garage. The door shut behind him and his shoes tapped on the concrete as he went down the aisle to his rental car. He had the key fob in hand as he reached the four-door.

"Stop, Raven."

The man didn't have to raise his voice.

Raven turned. The man with the handgun had stepped out of hiding from between a truck and a van. Two more joined him from other locations, each one holding a pistol on him. He wasn't going to punch his way out of this one.

"Put the bag down."

Raven complied. The tote *clunked* onto the concrete floor. One of the other gunners rushed over, picked up the tote, and gestured for Raven to open his jacket. The man ripped the Nighthawk .45 from the speed rig and jammed the gun into his waistband.

A car came around a corner, the headlights bathing Raven and the other men in bright light. The car stopped. The gunmen shoved Raven toward the car. One opened the trunk. Before Raven had a chance to argue, somebody behind him smacked him over the head with an all-steel pistol. Raven felt his knees bend, but the lights went out before he crumpled to the ground.

45

CORD FOLLOWED THE VOICE COMMANDS AND DASH SCREEN map of the Peugeot's GPS and reached the location of Monique Choffron's hideout in 45 minutes. At least, the computer and Galeri's notes *said* he was there. All he saw on either side of the road were trees, with the lights of Versailles proper glowing in the distance.

He pulled the Peugeot into an opening off the road, took his tote into the darkness of the trees, and prepped by feel. His nine-millimeter auto was snug in a hip holster. He secured his armored chest rig, dropped spare mags for his Galil ACE into the pouches on either side, then lastly charged the Galil rifle itself. He didn't worry about the *clack-clack* of cranking the bolt.

Cord started forward, his eyes adjusting, but still feeling his way with left hand extended so he didn't collide with a tree trunk. The ground was full of overgrowth, dead leaves and pine needles. He set his feet down softly with each step. He paused 100 yards from the road to send a note to Galeri. Before he had a chance to seek cover, a voice said, "Stop."

Behind and to the left.

Cord dived right, crashing into a hollow fallen trunk; a burst of auto-fire split the trunk some more, the slugs punching the dirt inches from Cord's face as he landed on the other side. With the Galil pinned under him and the bad guy moving in, he snatched out the nine-millimeter, rolled onto his left arm, and aimed over the hollow log. He fired as his opponent dropped and rolled. Cord lost sight of the man, but heard the ground debris crunch as he scrambled to a new position. Cord holstered the pistol and hurried forward on his belly. Another burst of auto fire hit the ground where he'd been, one shot nicking the heel of his left boot.

The ground sloped. Cord rolled down, stopping against thick brush. A third burst split the air over his head, but at least he had his rifle ready for action. Cord returned fire, two single rounds, but stomping footsteps indicated no hits. Cord jumped to his feet and ran. What lay ahead he wasn't sure, but the uncertainly beat the hell out of the gunman behind him. He tripped on a fallen branch and tumbled into a ditch. Gasping, clutching his rifle close, he listened, ignoring the pain of the fall.

The gunman was talking as he tracked Cord's location. He kept his voice low but the sound traveled despite his precaution; it was a one-sided chat. He was calling home base to report the intruder and ask for backup.

Great. Where is Raven when I need him?

And where is Galeri and his men?

Cord rose slightly and fired at shadows. The gunman went silent. Cord dropped low and waited.

A noise. More boots cracking debris. Getting closer. But they weren't moving fast.

A burst from the gunman smacked a tree to Cord's left. He winced at the sound but stayed put.

Dried leaves crunched to Cord's right.

A trickle of sweat crawled from Cord's forehead to his jaw.

I'm surrounded.

But fighting in the dark, as one of his former combat instructors like to say, *sucks*. If you can't see, neither can they.

Cord turned and rolled up over the opposite site of the ditch, then slid forward on his belly. He stopped at the base of another tree.

He scanned the familiar shadows, the natural shapes. The tree cover was too thick to let any of the city light bleed through, and he waited for the outline of his opponent to break the natural line. The gunman might be holding still until backup arrived, but they had to have a recognition code, lights, or *something* useful to make sure they didn't shoot each other. What Cord wondered was why the new arrivals he heard hadn't tried to link up with their man.

Cord continued his scan. A noise on his left—

He turned too late.

The gunman loomed in front of him with his rifle lining up on Cord's face.

A flashlight beam struck. The man winced and put up an arm. Cord rolled as two shots cracked. When he looked where the gunman had stood, he instead saw where the man lay dead.

The light beam settled on Cord. A man rasped to another in harsh French not to shoot.

"It's me, Cord," the speaker then added. The light snapped off. Cord gratefully shook hands with the bearded Ike Galeri.

"Pretty close," Galeri said.

"Thanks. Who's your friend?"

Cord glanced at the shorter man beside Galeri, who nodded but kept a danger scan as the other two spoke.

"One of mine," Galeri said. "Call him Phil. Come on."

"Wait, that guy called for help."

"He's met them by now, in whatever chamber of hell they wound up. Thanks to him we've reduced Monique's troops by six. Where's Raven?"

"Separate car."

"He'll find us. Let's go."

Galeri took the lead with Cord in the middle. The man named Phil covered the rear.

46

RAVEN WOKE UP IN THE TRUNK. HE TRIED TO FIGHT THE nausea from the earlier blow to the head, but failed. There was nowhere to throw up except to the right, near the trunk lock. After, he had no way to avoid getting the results on his clothes. And the smell overpowered the pungent exhaust.

At least the ride wasn't bumpy. The enemy had the forethought to select a smooth-riding car to drive to whichever out of the way grave they'd already dug. Maybe they weren't such bad chaps, after all.

They'd also failed to restrain him. Raven felt around in the dark for a potential weapon. The trunk was empty, but for him and a pile of runny vomit soaking his clothes. Oh, the glamor.

A green glow caught his eye. It was the emergency release handle near the trunk lock. He *could* pull it and escape, but they'd only pursue. And they had his gun. If he wanted a chance to get the pistol back, he needed to wait. He also decided there was a chance they'd bring him to Monique. She'd want to pull the trigger herself.

He hoped Cord and Galeri were okay.

The ride continued. Raven made his position as comfortable as possible and waited. He hoped his muscles didn't cramp too badly.

———————

THE CAR STOPPED.

Based on a series of turns over the last several minutes, Raven figured they were near their destination.

But nobody opened the trunk right away. There were people talking. Six of their men had vanished. One outer guard, and the five sent to help when he encountered an intruder. For all they knew, the house was surrounded. Somebody suggested they get the prisoner out. The sight of him might make his friends hesitate.

Raven waited. Remaining scrunched in a trunk in no way made one combat ready. There'd be no jumping out to fight this time. But he knew he wasn't alone in the wilderness. Cord and Galeri and Galeri's men were close.

The trunk latch clicked and a man with a sub gun raised the lid. Then he recoiled from the stink of vomit. Too bad, Raven thought, he couldn't leap out and engage in a furious martial arts battle like in the movies. He had the perfect distraction going for him.

The man backed away and aimed his weapon at Raven. He ordered him to get out. Two more gunners joined him. Lights from the side of a house lit the area, and the two gunners wore street clothes and running shoes. Raven took his time. He felt funny from the exhaust exposure and his legs ached. He carefully exited the trunk, and leaned against the car for support. The fresh air felt good and revived him.

One, two, four…six. Six gunners around him, around the car, and the light betrayed their kill-crazy faces. They wanted to rip Raven apart, and as he noted each face, he wondered what the chances of beating them might be. The war had to end sometime. He'd said so to Broularid to needle the old bastard, but if six men faced him now, how many more did he not see? What if he'd finally overplayed his hand? But he felt the presence of the locket around his neck, under his shirt; the ghosts of battles past wouldn't let him go so easily.

There was always a chance to win. He had to find one.

Or make one.

A gunner grabbed him and shoved him toward a door. Another gunner followed behind. The rest stayed outside and somebody switched off the light. The interior of the house was dim, the hallway they followed dark but for spillover from a larger room at the end.

They did not go to the lit room. The gunners tossed Raven into a room midway along the hall, and locked the door from the hallway side. He landed on soft carpet, and looked around after sitting up. Small bedroom. No bed. Empty closet. Nothing useful, same as the trunk. Great. And he didn't know which of the goons had his gun. He wanted it back. But the cramps in his legs and ache in his back were gone and they still hadn't restrained him. *There will be some American ninja action yet*, he decided.

Raven stood up to walk around, and felt along the wall for a light switch. He flicked it upward, and a light in the center of the ceiling bathed the room in brightness. He sat against the wall as far from the door as possible. All he needed was a baseball to bounce off the walls.

They made him wait five minutes.

The lock in the door clicked and Monique entered. The two gunmen who'd put Raven in the room followed. They held their submachine guns steady and ready.

Don't be an idiot. Wait.

"Hello, Raven."

"Your boss called me *Mister* Raven."

She scoffed.

"But I'm impressed. I only had to wait five minutes. Better than most doctors' offices."

Monique put her hands on her hips. She looked down at him. She seemed pleased. Gone was the skirt / blouse business attire; now she wore jeans, heavy-duty hiking boots, and a thick and slightly distracting sweater. For once, Raven had no trouble keeping his eyes from looking where men naturally glance.

"Chose your next joke carefully. It might be your last."

"Knock, knock," Raven said.

Her smile resembled a snarl; Raven was glad to finally see her up close. Then she was *really* close, because she came forward to stop inches from him. She extended her left leg.

"Like my boots?" she said.

All wit left Raven as he realized what optional extra her boots included.

"Steel toes," Monique said. She kicked him in the belly. Raven doubled over, trying to suck air, as the pain of the impact spread through his body.

She grabbed a handful of his hair and jerked his face up to meet hers.

"Any further remarks?"

Raven shook his head, his face red, still struggling to breathe, his choking gasps amusing Monique and the gunmen. She let go. Raven collapsed on the carpet. Monique stepped away. When Raven sat up again a few minutes later, breathing painfully but at least able to do so, the woman continued.

"Much better. Now. How many shooters did you bring?"

"You'll find out soon enough."

"But will you live long enough to see them?" Monique reached behind her back for a small pistol, a Walter PPK. She aimed at Raven's face.

Raven's upper lip twitched.

Now or never.

She cocked the Walther. The click of the hammer filled the room.

"Denosha and his wife are gone, and now you'll be gone. I'll deal with Noel Lalande *personally*, you have my word, *Mister* Raven."

Raven let her see a smile. If the cavalry was coming, they needed to show up *right now*.

The first crackle of gunfire came from far away, but produced immediate results. Men outside screamed in alarm, return fire popped louder; somebody began shouting orders.

Monique yelled, "Go!" to the men in the doorway without taking her eyes off Raven. The two gunners raced out.

Her finger tightened on the Walther's trigger.

And Raven made his move.

47

CORD, GALERI, AND GALERI'S TWO SHOOTERS HID IN THE TREE line at the edge of the property, where a field of grass met the forest. The house and surrounding structures sat on concrete. The field didn't interest Cord. Darkness covered that area, with all activity taking place around the house.

Cord and Galeri counted the men who exited the car and watch one open the trunk. Raven climbed out on wobbly legs, and leaned against the vehicle, only for one of the enemy gunners to shove him toward the house. A second gunner followed.

The house sat neat the back edge of the concrete square; to the left as one stood on the front porch, a pair of storage sheds stood side-by-side. Miscellaneous garden equipment lay against the wall of the one facing Cord. Across from the sheds, a garage, both sliding doors closed.

Two men took Raven into the house, leaving four more outside, and Cord felt, rather than sensed, their nervous tension. The snippets of conversation he picked up explained why. They were aware their comrades weren't coming back.

254 | BRIAN DRAKE

They knew an attack force waited in the forest. What they didn't know was how many they faced.

The gunner in charge directed his men to cover positions and the men slipped into various nooks, covered by shadows, but still easily seen. Galeri wore a set of night-vision goggles, and pointed out who was hiding where.

He whispered the words to his second shooter, whom he'd introduced only as "Bill". Cord figured Bill and the other man, Phil, didn't want their real names on record. Fair enough. But Bill carried a sniper rifle with a scope, itself night-vision capable, and he confirmed the enemy position as Galeri called them out.

"Let's do it," Galeri said.

Cord tucked his Galil ACE tightly to his shoulder.

Bill fired first.

The high-powered rifle let off a *whip-crack* as the round left the muzzle. A gunner near the garage toppled onto the pavement, his sub gun sliding across the concrete.

Cord, Galeri, and Phil opened fire with their automatic rifles, letting off short bursts in random patterns, the enemy gunners yelling to each other in response as they rallied to return fire at an opposing force they couldn't see.

Bill fired another round, dropping a gunman as he tried to run from the side of the garage to the car in which Raven had arrived. His body sprawled face down.

Cord tracked a gunman as he bent low and ran for one of the storage sheds. The Galil chattered against his shoulder, the burst stitching the man through the face and neck. He crashed into the yard equipment and knocked everything over, the crash overpowering the rapid pops of gunfire.

RAVEN SAT against the wall with his legs out in front of him. Lunging at Monique wasn't an option.

He threw his weight to the left instead, rolling away from the Walther's business end. Monique pivoted to track him, and squeezed off her shot too soon. As she swung the pistol at him again, he lunged, tackling her mid-body. Monique fell back with a scream, firing into the ceiling. She hit the floor on her back, the Walther flying from her hand. She clawed at Raven's face.

Raven winced as he nails dug into his skin, but he forced his arms between hers, and swept outward, breaking her grip, and, knees on either side of her, inched along her body to clamp both hands around her neck.

Her eyes went wide and a gurgled cry got lost in her throat. Raven leaned into the squeeze. She struggled against him and tried to bring up her knees to break his hold; he didn't let go. She clamped her hands on his wrists and dug her nails into his skin once more. Raven ignored the pain. He squeezed harder.

Somebody entered the room.

Monique's hopeful eyes flashed to the new arrival. Raven rolled off her as Ramon Crozier took aim with his pistol.

Ramon held his fire as Raven rolled left again, snatching Monique's fallen Walther. Coming up on his knees, he fired twice before Ramon found a sight picture. Ramon fell back against the wall and dropped onto the carpet.

Raven swung the PPK to Monique.

She was coughing, her face red, twisted with agony, as she stared down the muzzle of her own gun.

Raven pulled the trigger.

The Walther popped and sent a .380 ACP slug smack between her eyes. She flopped on the floor. Her body twitched, then lay still.

Automatic gunfire continued outside. Raven barely registered the sounds. He dropped the Walther and collected Ramon's HK .40-caliber autoloader. He found a spare magazine in Ramon's pants pocket. Stepping over the man's body, Raven paused in the doorway.

The shooting outside became sporadic; one final shot, sounding like a high-powered rifle, silenced a chattering sub gun, and the echoes of gunfire faded to silence. But Raven's pulse beat heavy in his head. Who won?

He waited.

A door opened somewhere down the hall; the side door Raven had been brought through. He tightened his grip on the HK pistol.

"Raven!"

Cord's voice.

"Raven, it's Cord!"

Raven let out a breath of relief.

"In the hall!" he called back. He stepped into the hall. Cord lowered his weapon and ran to him.

"You all right?"

"A few scratches. Any losses on our side?"

"Nope."

"Then let's get out of here."

They ran outside, where Galeri and his two shooters were checking bodies. Galeri approached holding a pistol with a familiar shape.

"Lose something, Raven?"

The bearded Frenchman held up the Nighthawk .45. Raven took the gun with a smile, and tossed the HK away.

RAVEN STEPPED out of the shower and toweled off. He'd left the bathroom door open, so no steam covered the mirrors. It felt good to be back at his hotel, to have some time to let the aches and pains depart, but he still had a lot on his mind. He leaned against the counter and examined his face in the mirror, but didn't register his reflection. Thoughts overpowered him. There was so much he still didn't understand about Dave and Jen, and he had to make peace with never knowing the answers. He wasn't sure how to do so.

The Lalandes, wherever they were hiding, were safe. Once the French federal agents moved on Broularid, they'd know it was okay to go home. There was solace in the hollow victory, at least. He'd kept them safe from those intent on destroying them.

But his job wasn't finished.

He still had a promise to keep.

Kayla Blaine waited for him in San Francisco.

48

THE NEXT MORNING, STILL TIRED BUT READY TO GO, RAVEN walked across the lobby carrying his suitcases. A man stood in the busy lobby and waved him over. Raven didn't smile. Bruno Brunelle, the French federal cop, suggested they find a place to sit. They took a seat on the outer edge of the lobby, a place good for people watching, but Raven tuned out everything around him. He wanted to know what the federal cop had to tell him.

"You have a few scratches," Brunelle said.

"They'll heal."

"The rest of you?"

"We'll see."

"Well, I wish you luck. We arrested Broularid this morning. He complained we interrupted his breakfast." Brunelle laughed. "The next breakfast he has will be in a holding cell."

"You have enough to make it stick?"

"Kidnapping charges for one, and a witness, as you know. The audio you provided is good, too. Then your CIA pals made good on their promise. They found interesting connections on Broularid's cell phone, and we're in the process of showing Mr. Broularid how futile it is to resist. We expect the usual legal shenanigans, of course. But I think he's going away for a long time."

"If not, call me."

Brunelle laughed without humor. "I had a feeling you'd say something similar. Have a good flight back to the States, Mr. Raven." He stood. Raven stood. Brunelle held out a hand and Raven shook. "France thanks you for your help."

"Anytime."

Raven picked up his suitcase, turned, and walked away. He wanted to put Paris behind him, far behind, and not come back for a long time.

———

CALLEN CORD ENTERED the Dulles terminal with his carry-on, and proceeded through the crowd to baggage claim. While waiting for his suitcase on the carousel, Clark Wilson found him. The two men shook hands.

"Thanks for the pickup," Cord said.

"Least I could do. Have you talked to Sam?"

Cord shook his head. "I tried to talk to him, but he wouldn't answer his phone. I guess he cut me off."

"Don't take it personally. This job was tough on him."

"Well, it would have been nice to say good-bye."

"You'll see him again. I have a feeling. Before you know it."

"You have something in mind?"

"Grab your bag and we'll talk in the car."

Cord knew when to shut up. He did as he was told, and followed Wilson out to the parking lot.

WILSON DROVE ONTO THE BELTWAY. Traffic inched along.

"Let's hear it," Cord said.

"Broularid's phone. My guys hacked it. We found his CIA contact is, a man named Masen Walsh. Works on the seventh floor. He had access to all the reports I filed regarding you and Raven and everything in Paris."

"Uh-huh."

"My boss has decided we're going to let him dangle. FBI has him under surveillance, and they've started coordinating with authorities in Paris. If he tries to flee the country, they'll pounce. He's been working at home since news of the arrest broke, and he hasn't gone anywhere, nor made any calls."

"They need to bring him in," Cord said. "Maybe he knows something about the Denosha murders here. Hell, he might have helped organize the hit."

"We'll find out."

"Can't wait."

"Are you disappointed? I figured you'd want to have a chat with him yourself."

"There's been enough killing for a while," Cord said. "I'm with Raven. You gotta hit the pause button sometime."

"True."

Wilson drove on.

———

IT WAS late in the day when Raven landed at SFO, but renewed energy surged as he sat in the back of the cab and sped along Highway 101 into San Francisco. The cab took him downtown to the hotel where Roger Justice and Lia Kenisova still kept Kayla in protective custody. He was jumpy and nervous when he stopped in front of the hotel room door. Yes, he wanted to keep his commitment, take some time away from the life he led. He deserved a break.

But he had to fight the instinct to run. Run to the next fight. Someday he hoped he learned how to really rest.

He knocked.

Lia answered.

"Hey, boss!" she shouted. She let Raven into the suite. Roger came over to say hello, but never got a word out. Kayla pushed him aside as she ran into Raven's arms. They hugged each other tight. He wanted to kiss her, but not in front of witnesses.

"Told you I'd be back," he said.

"I knew you would."

They didn't let go of each other.

A LOOK AT: VENGEANCE STRIKE: A SAM RAVEN THRILLER

BY BRIAN DRAKE

Betrayal puts Sam Raven on a course for revenge.

It was the kind of job Raven couldn't turn down. A daughter dead from a drug overdose, a father who wants the man responsible dead —and not only the street pushers. Kendrick Ward wants the *cartel boss* responsible removed from existence. Raven agrees, and he and his team of mercenaries fly into Colombia. Mission: kill narco boss Martin Sevilla and crush his empire.

But when the job is done, Ward pulls a double cross, and makes a big mistake. Only Raven survives the ambush.

Now Raven is ready to give back twice as much as received. He crashes through the heart of the betrayal to find a conspiracy of epic proportions, American Big Business and other cartel bosses working hand-in-hand. Raven's fighting a war without end, and the circle of violence spares no one. It's go time.

AVAILABLE OCTOBER 2025

ABOUT THE AUTHOR

A twenty-five year veteran of radio and television broadcasting, Brian Drake has spent his career in San Francisco where he's filled writing, producing, and reporting duties with stations such as KPIX-TV, KCBS, KQED, among many others. Currently carrying out sports and traffic reporting duties for Bloomberg 960, Brian Drake spends time between reports and carefully guarded morning and evening hours cranking out action/adventure tales.

A love of reading when he was younger inspired him to create his own stories, and he sold his first short story, "The Desperate Minutes," to an obscure webzine when he was 25 (more years ago than he cares to remember, so don't ask).

Brian Drake lives in California with his wife and two cats, and when he's not writing he is usually blasting along the back roads in his Corvette with his wife telling him not to drive so fast, but the engine is so loud he usually can't hear her.

briandrakebooks.com

www.ingramcontent.com/pod-product-compliance
Lightning Source LLC
Chambersburg PA
CBHW021252280626
47169CB00021B/2961